CW00554016

Oxygen

Elise Noble

To MJ

from

Elise Noble

Published by Undercover Publishing Limited

Copyright © 2016 Elise Noble

ISBN: 978-1-910954-17-1

This book is a work of fiction. Names and characters are the product of the author's imagination and any resemblance to actual persons, living or dead, is entirely coincidental.

All rights reserved. No part of this book may be reproduced or transmitted in any form or by any means, electronic or mechanical, including photocopying, recording, or by any information storage and retrieval system, without permission in writing from the author.

Edited by Amanda Ann Larson

Cover art by Abigail Sins

www.undercover-publishing.com

www.elise-noble.com

For PianomanTim, for cheering me up on a rainy evening, for bringing positivity into the world, and for charming those keys.

CHAPTER 1

MY FINGERS FLEW over the piano keys as I played Beethoven's Sonata No. 14 in C-sharp minor through for the third time. Well, the third time that morning. An old treasure, it was one of my go-to pieces when I was feeling down. I'd been playing it more and more often lately.

As I started the second movement, the allegretto, my mother stuck her head around the door, smiling as always. "Akari, would you like tea?"

"Yes please, Okasan."

Drinking tea had become our morning ritual since I moved back to Japan. Every morning at eleven, my mother would ask exactly the same thing, and my answer would never be any different. I'd smile politely, drink the delicately perfumed matcha she poured, then go back to my practice.

I'd just finished my fourth rendition of Beethoven when she laid the tea-making utensils out on the tatami mat on the other side of the music room. My favourite place in the apartment, it was where I spent most of my time and the reason I'd chosen the penthouse in Hiroo in the first place. Well, that and the view. Floor-to-ceiling windows looked out over homes belonging to the rich and famous in neighbouring Azabu, and at times it felt like I could see half of Tokyo, the city I'd once thought of as home.

Before I sat down, I checked on my baby, still asleep in his crib in the corner. Although at a year old, I wouldn't be able to call Hisashi that for much longer. Every day he seemed to get bigger.

At first I'd worried about playing the piano with him in the room, relying on the damper pedal to take the edge off the volume. But I'd soon found out he didn't mind. In fact, even the more raucous pieces made him drop off faster than if I simply rocked him in my arms. I guess he inherited my love of music, which right now seemed to be the only genes we shared. To look at, he was the spitting image of his father, something that made me happy and sad at the same time. Happy because a small part of him lived on in our son. Sad because every time I looked at Hisashi, he reminded me of what I'd lost.

I hitched up my silk pants and knelt on a mat opposite my mother. Nothing changed—she'd spent years mastering the art of the Japanese tea ceremony while I was a child, and she still liked to practice on me.

"Your playing gets more beautiful every day," she said, sliding a plate of mochi toward me.

The glutinous rice cakes had never been a love of mine, but I shrugged and took one anyway. "It's just practice. I still have so much to learn."

"Is Nomura-sensei coming today?"

I nodded. "At four."

As he did every Tuesday and Friday. Another perk of having money now was being able to afford lessons with the best piano teacher in Tokyo, although I'd give up every dollar in a heartbeat if it brought Hisashi's father back.

"I'll finish cleaning before then, so I can look after Hisashi."

"Thank you."

The apartment was spotless, as always. Cleaning formed another regular part of my mother's day. My father insisted on working, even though he no longer needed to, while Okasan was content to stay at home most of the time.

"Are you going out today?" she asked.

"To the park, after lunch."

Apart from the odd shopping trip, my daily walk was the only escape I got from the apartment, always following a different route.

I picked up the dainty china bowl, hand painted with colourful birds, and raised it to my lips. I'd had that same bowl since I was a child, and my parents had kept it ever since. Oh, how different my world was since the day I first used it. But not Okasan's tea. The sweet, grassy aroma floated up at me as I sipped. When I first got kidnapped, all those years ago, I'd missed such simple things, dreamed of them every night. My mother's voice waking me up in the morning. My father sitting straight-backed at the head of the table at dinner. The constant irritation of my little brother as he asked questions about anything and everything.

But as the years passed, the memories faded. I'd spent more of my time on this earth held prisoner than with my own family, and while I tried my best to slot back into my old life, they felt like strangers to me.

My father was easiest to deal with. He left for work at seven, returning from the factory late in the afternoon. My mother and brother? They were a different story.

Before I could take another mouthful of tea, my phone rang. Again.

"Hiro?" In reality, I didn't need to ask who was calling. Only a handful of people ever phoned me, and ninety percent of the time it was my brother on the other end of the line.

"Just checking everything's okay."

"I haven't left the house since you went to work."

"Good. That's good. Do you want me to pick anything up from the store?"

"No, there's nothing I need." Apart from some space, but no matter how many hints I dropped, he wouldn't give me any. I understood why—when your little sister got snatched from the street in broad daylight at the age of thirteen, it was only natural to get a bit overprotective, but that didn't make it any easier to take.

"I'll call you this afternoon, okay? If you think of anything, all you need to do is let me know."

"I will, I promise." I tossed the phone back on the table and sighed.

"Your brother's a good boy," Okasan said. "He cares about you."

"I know," I said, but my tone must have belied my words.

"He only worries. We all do. Nobody wants to see you go through such a...horrible experience again."

We'd never really spoken about it, what happened. Okasan didn't want to hear about it, and I didn't want to put it into words, not again.

I'd done it once, and that was bad enough. The people who rescued me were the only ones who knew the whole story. Hiro tried sending me to a therapist when we got back to Japan, but I hated every second of my time with her. The intrusive questions asked in a soft voice. The patronising words framed as kindness. Apparently, I over-analysed everything and needed to let myself grieve. After half a dozen visits I'd come home, cried into my pillow for an hour, then cancelled the rest of my sessions. Hiro's scowl, quickly hidden, told me what he thought of my decision, but it was my life, not his. I wouldn't be going again.

My father never asked about my time in Colombia, either. Denial trumped knowledge in his world. He was simply happy to have me back. So many people told me that he'd never smiled while I was gone, but these days, sunshine lit his eyes.

"What happened was a one-off, Okasan. Nobody wants to take me again, not now. I'm too old."

She smiled her gentle smile. "You're still my little girl. Don't let your tea get cold."

The temperature outside was warm enough for me to leave my jacket behind as I tucked Hisashi into his stroller. Up until a few weeks ago I'd carried him in a sling, but now he'd got too heavy. I'd finally given in and switched to a stroller, and I missed having him close.

"The park again?" asked Daiki, stepping forward from his spot to the side of the front door in the lobby.

I nodded. My life was nothing but predictable. He held the door open for me to go through then followed along behind. Daiki was one of my regular bodyguards, and I'd got to know him well over the past year. He'd confided that although minding me was a little dull, at least he knew he'd get home on time each evening. His son was a few months older than Hisashi, so I understood how important it was for Daiki to see him grow up.

Out of the corner of my eye, I glimpsed another of my security detail on the other side of the street. He was a younger man, slim, who moved with the power and grace of a leopard. I didn't know his name, and I wasn't sure I wanted to. He scared me.

The guards came courtesy of Hisashi's father. Or rather, his family. After he died, they swore to look after me and his son, and they'd kept their word. They ran a security company called Blackwood, and keeping people safe was their mission in life. At first the protection was my security blanket, the thing that let me sleep at night, but lately that cover had started to smother me.

A young boy whizzed by me on roller skates, making me jump. Daiki's hand went straight to his pocket, his frame tense and ready, before he relaxed once more. I stroked the soft fuzz on Hisashi's head, whispering it would be okay, but my reassurances were for my benefit rather than his. He simply babbled non-words and smiled his father's smile.

One lap of Arisugawa park, then two. On the way past the bench at the far end, I paused to drop a hundred yen into a beggar's cup. It was the only part of my route that remained constant. As he always did, he thanked me politely then resumed his broken stare. Somehow, seeing him there each day made me feel better. Not just that I'd helped him a little, but because he served as a reminder to be grateful for my own life. I should be happy. I had a family who loved me, a beautiful home, and a son who gave me a reason to get up in the mornings.

So why did I feel trapped?

The first fat plops of rain fell as we reached the exit of the park. I fiddled with the stroller's hood as Daiki leapt forward with an umbrella and held it over Hisashi and me, not caring about getting wet himself.

"It's my job to keep you dry," he'd told me in the past when I offered to share.

I hurried my steps, anxious to get home before the rain worsened and soaked him. By the time we reached my apartment building, my mood, so grey of late, had turned as black as the clouds above me.

CHAPTER 2

"AGAIN. THOSE EIGHT bars should be thunderous. Fortissimo means very loud, not half-hearted," Nomura-sensei said.

Craving my mentor's approval, I tried the middle section of the Bach piece again, his Toccata and Fugue. I longed to play it on an organ one day as Bach intended, rather than a piano, but no matter what, I still loved the composition. Okasan didn't enjoy the darker music I sometimes channelled, but she'd taken Hisashi out to sit on the terrace, so I had free rein to play as I chose.

"Better. Now once more, from the beginning."

Sensei drilled me through the music three more times before we switched to Mozart then finished up with something by The Beatles, played by ear. By the time I lifted my hands from the keys, he was shaking his head.

"Your talent is wasted in here, Akari-san. You should allow others to hear your gift."

"I'm not good enough for that."

I'd taken six months of piano lessons as a five-year-old, enough to understand the basics of reading music, but apart from that I was self-taught. There simply wasn't the money for lessons every week. I listened to the radio, then copied each song on the old upright piano my father had worked overtime every week for three months to buy. Okasan would listen to me play then bring me tea. See what I mean when I said nothing changed?

As a child I'd dreamed of attending the Tokyo University of Music to learn the craft properly, and I'd practised every day in the hope of winning a scholarship. Then in my second year of junior high, that dream was snatched away, and I didn't play a note for fifteen years. No, I still had a lot to learn.

"Then have you considered my suggestion?"

A month ago, after I'd played "Bohemian Rhapsody" in four different keys, Sensei asked whether I'd thought about going to college.

"I've been away for too long. I missed out on five years of schooling, and you know how important that is in this country."

Children competed from kindergarten for places at the best universities, and not only had I missed nearly all of high school, I'd forgotten most of what I'd learned at elementary as well. In South America I'd discovered how to survive, but beyond speaking Spanish fluently, little of my knowledge would benefit me in the cutthroat education system.

"What about a different country?"

My jaw dropped. "I only just got home. I can't leave again."

"Why not? I am an old man, and I will not be able to teach you forever. Besides, your natural ability far surpasses mine. You need the right teacher to help coax it out of you."

I shook my head. "My parents would never leave Tokyo."

"You could go by yourself."

"I can't."

"Why not?"

How did I explain I'd never done anything alone? My whole life, I'd been surrounded by people, from my parents to my abductors. Yes, I'd hated being treated as a slave, but over the years I'd grown numb to it. The rapes, the beatings, the way men treated me as an object to be passed around—it became life. I stopped waking up every morning and wishing for things to be different because I didn't believe they ever would be. Then when I'd given up hope, Hisashi's father helped me see the silver lining in a world of black clouds.

And in all that time, I'd never been on my own. I'd never needed to make decisions, or hold any responsibility, or set my own schedule. Nothing scared me more.

"I just can't."

Sensei took my hands, so pale because I rarely saw the sun, in his wizened fingers. Long and slender, even in his mid-seventies few could play the piano better than him. The idea that he thought I would one day be able to was almost as far-fetched as me leaving Japan.

"Promise me, Akari, promise me you'll think about it. Don't give up on your dreams. Otherwise there will come a time when you'll look back and regret what might have been."

His plea was so honest, so heartfelt I couldn't turn him down. "I promise."

After all, thinking couldn't hurt, could it?

Two months later, the first sakura trees began to blossom. As I stood in the cemetery, Hisashi in my arms and my family by my side, I marvelled at the delicate pink flowers that swayed in a gentle breeze. In the rainforest where I'd spent so much time, the trees had been a wall of green, impenetrable and foreboding. Here, their foliage, from green to red to golden to brown in the autumn, offered a world of possibilities, and the new buds in spring symbolised life. And now, to me, death.

Nomura-sensei's last wish was that he should be laid to rest in the Aoyama cemetery, beside his wife of fifty-four years, and despite the tears I couldn't stop, I needed to be there to see it happen. Hiro handed me another tissue as the urn containing Sensei's ashes was slid into a chamber under the freshly engraved stone monument.

My teacher's death came as a shock to me, but not to him. I'd noticed him looking a little tired over the months he'd been visiting, but with no reason to suspect anything sinister, I'd put it down to late nights and the changing seasons. Then one day, he didn't arrive for my lesson. My phone calls went unanswered, and the next day his son came to see me instead.

"I wanted to be the one to tell you," he started, and straight away I knew my mentor had left us. It wasn't Takuma's black suit, or the handkerchief he clutched in his hands, but his eyes. They'd lost the playful glint that had danced in them when I first met him, at his mother's birthday party soon after I moved into my apartment. "It's... It's..."

I took his cold hands in mine, trying to add what little strength I possessed to them. "I'm so sorry."

"I've had some time to prepare, but still I can't believe he's gone."

"How did he...?"

"Cancer. He fought it for years, and when it came back last May, he refused further treatment. My father wished to die with dignity rather than prolong the inevitable."

Last May. Just a month after I first met him. "I wish he'd told me. I could have done things differently."

"That was exactly why he didn't. When he was with you, it allowed him to escape from his body into his mind. He always said you played like an angel."

"I'm not sure we heard the same notes."

"You need to have more confidence in yourself." He freed one of his hands to fish around in his jacket pocket. "My father asked me to give you this."

As I reached out for the envelope, the tears I'd been fighting escaped, cascading down my cheeks and splashing onto the wooden floor Okasan lovingly polished every other morning. I wiped them away with my sleeve, but it was a pointless task. The river would never stop.

After Takuma left with a stiff bow, I ran to Hisashi's nursery and snatched him up into my arms. The tears kept coming, not only for my teacher but for a father who'd never see his son grow up.

An hour passed, then two. At first, I cradled my son in the rocking chair by the window, but as he fidgeted more I laid his *Under the Sea* play set out on the floor and sat with him as he threw the cuddly sea creatures around. Try as I might, I couldn't giggle with him. The whole time, the envelope I'd placed on the small table that held Hisashi's toy box watched me. Finally, I could bear it no longer. I needed to know what it said.

My name was written on the outside in Sensei's flowing script, still neat despite the disease that ravaged his body: *Akari Takeda*. Hands trembling, I pulled out a single sheet of paper and paced as I read.

Akari-San,

By the time you read this I'll have left you, and I need to apologise for keeping you in the dark over my condition. I didn't want to be defined by an event out of my control - I know this is something you will understand.

He was right there. My continual refusal to tell the police or the press what happened to me during their fifteen-year hunt invited the wrath of the former and the curiosity of the latter. While my bodyguards frustrated me at times, the thought of going out unprotected, leaving myself at the mercy of reporters, wasn't something I could consider. My abduction would be a weight round my neck for the rest of my life.

Not so long ago, you promised to consider the possibility of continuing your musical education at college, but as the words left your mouth your eyes spoke differently. Without encouragement, I know you'll spend the rest of your life locked up in Tokyo.

So I took it upon myself to give you that push. Two weeks after that conversation, I sent a video of you playing to the principal of the Holborn Conservatory. After extensive research, I firmly believe this to be the best place in the world for a budding pianist to learn her craft.

He did what? The recordings he made in my lessons were supposed to be for our ears only, so I could remind myself where I needed to make improvements. How dare he send something so private to a person I'd never met? Teeth clenched, I read on.

If the principal looks upon you favourably and offers you a place, I urge you to take it. If you can open your mind to new possibilities, I believe, no... I know, that nobody will be able to touch you when it comes to creating magic with a piano. Nobody dances with the keys as you do.
  I wish you all the luck in the world.
  Kosuke Nomura.

I wanted to be angry with him for interfering in my life, but the part of me I hated to listen to admitted he was right. Left to my own devices, I'd never get beyond the city limits. But the Holborn school? I didn't even know where that was.

Hisashi let out a cry, unhappy that my attention was focused elsewhere, and I rocked him in my arms until he settled again. Careful not to disturb him, I sat back down and pulled my phone out my pocket. It was time for some research.

CHAPTER 3

FROM THAT DAY on, I changed my routine slightly. Instead of settling on the stool to practise as soon as Hisashi went down for his morning nap, I took a trip to the lobby first to pick up the mail.

Not because I was expecting anything to come of Sensei's crazy application, more because I didn't want Okasan to see the rejection letter. She'd automatically assume it was me who'd wanted to leave, not my teacher who'd decided my path.

After all, rejection was inevitable. I'd snuck a look at the school's website one evening when Hisashi couldn't sleep, and attending would be any musician's dream. Located in Boston, the conservatory was founded in the 1980s after an endowment from a wealthy industrialist. The money enabled them to offer each student a full scholarship while they were taught to play their chosen instrument to a world-class standard. I'd spent most of that night watching videos of their performances, and the magic of Bach, Liszt and Chopin almost sent my soul straight to Haneda airport to get on a plane.

One look at my now-sleeping baby acted as brakes on that dream, though. That and an internet search revealing the school's rate of acceptance was just ten percent, or around twenty-five students a year. I had more chance of playing for the emperor than I did of getting a live audition.

Then the letter arrived.

A slim cream envelope, not unlike the one Sensei left me, although that one lay dog-eared in my desk while this one had a Boston postmark. The instant I grasped it in my hand, I half-ran to the elevator and jabbed the button, ignoring Daiki's curious glance.

The elevator rose slowly, far too slowly. The child in me wanted to rip the envelope open and get it over with, but I forced myself to wait. The thing was, I couldn't make up my mind what I wanted the letter to say. The easy option would be a flat no, and I could stick with my safe, easy life in Tokyo. My dull life. My boring, lonely life.

But there was a part of me, one planted as a small seed by Sensei which had grown and spread over the past few weeks, and that part wished for acceptance and the chance for a different life.

In the sanctuary of my bedroom, I quickly checked on Hisashi in the attached nursery then perched on the edge of my bed. Fingers trembling, I unpeeled the flap of the envelope, extracted the two thick sheets of paper inside, and began to read.

Dear Miss Takeda,

Thank you for applying to the Holborn Conservatory. Although we wouldn't usually accept students who have not completed high school, it was clear from the accompanying recommendation and recording that we should give your application further consideration.

We would therefore like to invite you to attend an

assessment day at our campus in Boston on August 12th. As well as a live audition before a committee of faculty members, your knowledge of music theory and ear training will be reviewed by one of our teachers, and you will need to take an essay writing exam. The day will finish with an interview with one of our senior administrators.

The dean's signature ended the letter with a flourish, and I flipped to the second page. It gave more details of the time and place and included a list of hotels in the area, making the situation all the more real.

Boston.

I'd only spent a few months in North America, Virginia to be precise, and I'd been surrounded by my family. The thought of making the journey alone terrified me, especially in just two short weeks.

But as I sat down at my Steinway grand a few minutes later, and my fingers went to the keys like it was where they belonged, the voice in my head I'd ignored for so long told me I had to try. *If you stay in Tokyo, you'll be the same nothing you've always been.* After a botched attempt at Debussy and an awkward cup of tea with my mother, I came to the conclusion I needed to talk to somebody about the problem. But who?

Not my family, and not that awful therapist. There was only one man. He'd told me to call him any time, night or day, but I rarely picked up the phone. Hisashi's uncle had his own life, and if not for the bizarre twist of fate that threw us together, our paths would never have crossed. Still, as a kind and patient man, I knew he'd listen to what I had to say without judgement.

"It's Akari," I said when he picked up the phone.

"Is everything all right?"

He had to know there was nothing physically wrong —Daiki would call him in a heartbeat if there was a problem. "Yes. Well, I'm not sure. I have a...dilemma."

Over the next few minutes, it all spilled out— Sensei's death, my worries about the future, the fear of hurting my family and finally, the offer from Boston. "I can't decide what to do. I'm scared to go to Boston, but I'm also scared not to."

"Where do you see yourself in five years' time?"

"I don't know. I never think of the future." The one time I'd dared to, I'd hoped for a life with Hisashi's father and that dream had been destroyed.

"You need to change that mindset. If you don't have a goal, you'll drift through life until it's too late, then you'll look back and wonder what you could have achieved if you'd only tried."

"So you think I should go?"

"I think you should decide what you want out of life and go all out to get it."

Silence stretched between us as I reflected on his words. In five years, ten, did I want to be sitting in this same room? My brother would be at work, Hisashi would be in fifth grade, and my parents would be in their seventies. I could easily waste a decade through inertia.

And in twenty years? My brother would surely meet a girl and marry, Hisashi would be at university and my parents...well, nobody lived forever, I knew that all too well. If I didn't change my path, I'd still be here, playing the piano and staring out at a changing skyline I played no part in.

"How do I book a flight?" I asked softly.

CHAPTER 4

THE FLIGHT BOOKED for me came with extra legroom and all the canapés I could eat. Daiki drove us to the airport, a sad smile on his face.

My mother, of course, surpassed that. She dabbed at her eyes with a handkerchief as she stood between the stoic frames of my father and brother, and I almost cancelled my ticket.

Instead, I shifted Hisashi into one arm and gave her a hug. "I'll be back next week. You'd better have the tea waiting."

"And then you will leave again."

"I doubt that. Chances are I won't be good enough."

"Of course they will want you. As soon as they hear you play, they will offer you a place."

I wished I shared her conviction. Locusts hopped in my stomach, and I wasn't sure whether to be nervous or excited. "We'll see."

She turned away. "I already know."

My brother tucked an arm around my shoulders. "The thought of losing you again is just hard for her."

And him. He'd spent most of yesterday trying to convince me not to go, and every day before that. He started off gently by explaining how much they'd all miss me. When I didn't change my mind, he looked up the crime statistics in Boston and tried to scare me into staying. And yesterday, when I said I still wanted to go, he played dirty and fetched my therapist.

I knew he meant well, but didn't he understand pulling stunts like that only made me want to leave more? I'd always love my brother, but I couldn't live with his constant over-protectiveness. Not truly live, with the freedom I'd craved for so many years.

I tried, and failed, to hold back a sigh as he made his final stand—the guilt trip at the airport.

"She's not losing me. I'll call her every day, I promise."

Hiro turned away from me, unhappy, and I tried to placate him.

"I'll call you too."

Nothing.

My father took my free hand, his face blank. "We are proud of you, Akari, but that does not make your departure easier."

"I know, Otasan. But I need to do this."

He let go of my hand and took a step back. "*Ganbatte.*" Do your best.

I nodded, my own eyes filling with tears. Of course I would.

Hisashi cried as the airplane took off, and I had to endure glares from the other passengers in first class. As I'd only be away for a few days, I'd considered leaving him at home with my parents but every time I imagined boarding the plane without him, I felt sick. He had to stay by my side.

As the pressure settled so did he, and he was soon

sleeping peacefully in my lap. On the whole he was a good child, although now he'd started walking I knew it was only a matter of time before he began causing trouble. Even now he was curious about everything, and he'd already managed to grip onto the flight attendant's scarf with surprising strength before I unpeeled his tiny fingers.

The thirteen-hour flight seemed to take twice that, mainly because I spent the duration worrying. Despite practising my audition pieces for the last two weeks solid, I had an irrational fear of forgetting the notes, not to mention my worry about the interview afterwards. English was my third language, and I'd barely needed to speak it for the past year.

At least Hisashi's Aunt Emmy had agreed to come to Boston for a few days to help me prepare. She'd promised to arrange a piano and somewhere for me to stay as well. Although I felt guilty for pulling her away from her life and job, I hadn't protested too hard when she offered to join me. At least I wouldn't be alone.

Despite several hours' sleep, I was exhausted as I carried Hisashi off the plane. My skin felt dry, my throat parched. I longed to get to whatever hotel we were staying in and get some more rest, even if my son didn't share that sentiment. His eyes darted all over the place, drinking in the hustle and bustle of a land he was too young to remember.

I soon spotted Emmy hanging over the railing in the arrivals lounge, a large paper cup of coffee in her hands. When I'd stayed with her, she'd started every morning with caffeine and as it was only half past seven in the US, it stood to reason she needed her fix.

With a baby in one hand and a suitcase in the other,

I couldn't wave, but she saw me straight away and raised an arm.

"How was the flight?" She spoke in Japanese.

I stifled a yawn. "Long. Do you mind if we talk in English? I need the practice."

"Sure," she replied in her British accent. "You can go back to bed when we get to where we're staying. The drive shouldn't take long. Here, give me the case."

She was right about the journey being quick. I'd almost forgotten how fast she drove, but with a child in the car I was pleased to note she toned it down a bit. Even so, we still pulled into the driveway of a large, detached house before nine o'clock.

"We're staying here? Not a hotel?"

"We struggled to find a hotel with a private practice room. This place comes with a Schimmel grand and a hot tub."

I had no need for the jacuzzi, but I couldn't manage without a piano. "Thank you for arranging it. If you let me know how much, I'll wire you the money."

"Don't worry about it. You're family."

Before I could insist, a neon-clad figure bounded out the front door and down the steps. "Bradley's here?"

She rolled her eyes. "I couldn't stop him. He's been up half the night installing a nursery."

"But we're only here for a week."

"You think that matters?"

Bradley, Emmy's assistant, enveloped me in a hug then plucked Hisashi from my grasp. He let out a howl, but when I tried to take him back, Bradley waved me away.

"We're fine." He cooed down at Hisashi. "Do you

remember your Auntie Bradley? Do you?"

My son unscrewed his face and made a grab for a Bradley's diamond earring. He loved sparkly things.

"See? All good." Bouncing him on his hip, Bradley set off back to the house, muttering something about Noah and cuddly toys.

"He's bought him a Noah's Ark?"

"You're lucky I talked him out of hiring real animals."

Emmy hauled my suitcase out of the trunk of the Ford Explorer, leaving me with only Hisashi's changing bag to carry. I never bothered with a separate handbag —so rare were my trips out that I just shoved my wallet and phone into a pocket. Not quite sure what to do with myself, I followed her inside.

The wood panelling on the walls made the house look gloomy, but I was pleased to find the music room was at the back, with tall windows overlooking the garden. I tapped a few of the keys and the rich sound of the German-made instrument filled the room.

"You want me to stick around?" Emmy asked. "Or can I shoot into the office?"

"You have a Boston branch?" Dumb question. Blackwood had offices everywhere from London to Tokyo. Of course they'd have several in the US.

"Yeah, a half hour away. Bradley'll stay and help with Hisashi, and there're a couple of guards around."

"Where? I didn't see them."

"Kitchen and spare bedroom." She looked at her watch then tilted her head on one side expectantly.

"Oh, it's fine. I can manage here. I'll need to practise for most of the day, anyway."

"See you at dinner, then."

It wasn't long before I heard the roar of the SUV heading up the driveway, and I sat down on the plush leather seat in front of the piano. Alone with only my thoughts and music for company, I began to play.

I must have repeated those four pieces a hundred times each over the past four days, but it paid off. Under the hawk-like gaze of five faculty members, I got through them all with only one small mistake in the Chopin étude, and even that I managed to cover up.

While my fingers flew over the keys they stayed steady, but as the room fell silent and I turned to face my audience, my hands shook. The easy part, the music, was over. Now I had to get through the interview. What if they hated me?

"So what made you choose the Holborn Conservatory, Miss Takeda?" the dean asked. "Your application was a little vague on that."

It would help if I knew what Sensei wrote, but as he hadn't told me I had to bluff it. Recalling Emmy's advice, I made eye contact and tried to smile. "Its reputation. Holborn has turned out so many world class musicians over the last decade, and I'd love to be one of them."

"There are a number of excellent schools in Japan. Why not go to one of those? Moving to Boston would be a big step, especially as I understand you have a young son?"

How could I explain that Boston represented a fresh start away from prying eyes that still saw me as a newspaper story? In Tokyo I'd never be free to live my life without questions, but in Boston maybe, just maybe... "I need to expand my cultural horizons, and I'd love to gain knowledge I could take back home with me at the end of my degree."

"Have you considered your options for childcare?"

"I would employ a nanny."

I'd thought about it over and over, and although it would be hard to spend time away from my son, in years to come the sacrifice could lead to a better life for us both.

The dean nodded, seemingly satisfied with my answer, and one of his colleagues took over, grilling me on music theory and my likes and dislikes for almost an hour. By the time I escaped from the room, weariness had taken the place of the locusts, and I sagged onto a bench outside.

"How'd it go?" Emmy materialised from nowhere and sat down beside me. I'd long since given up wondering how she did that.

"Okay, I think. It's hard to tell."

She passed me a sandwich—pastrami on rye. She knew that was my favourite and it wasn't easy to get hold of in Japan. "You'll get in. No problem."

It turned out she was right, as usual. I'd barely touched down on Japanese soil when my phone rang.

"Upon careful consideration, we'd like to offer you a full scholarship to join us for the next three years," said the dean.

It was a good thing I was sitting down because I'd surely have ended up on the floor otherwise. "I-I-I'm not quite sure what to say."

"Would you like us to hold the place for you?"

My future stood on one simple word: Yes, or no. If I said no, life would be easy, but "yes" held such potential, such power. The journey would be fraught with difficulty, but I had to make it anyway, otherwise I'd spend the rest of my life regretting my cowardice. "Yes, please. And thank you."

His voice took on a warmer tone, making him sound friendlier than before. "I'm very glad to hear that. We'll send an information pack out and our administrators will be happy to answer any questions you may have. I look forward to seeing you in four weeks."

Four weeks. Four weeks? I really hadn't thought this through properly, had I? How was I supposed to move from one side of the world to the other, find a place to live and arrange a nanny all within a month?

I clutched the phone, ready to call the dean back and tell him I'd made a mistake. But when I scrolled through my list of numbers, I ended up dialling Emmy instead.

CHAPTER 5

I'D BEEN EXPECTING Emmy to meet me in Boston, but when I got out to the arrivals lounge I found Bradley flanked by two taller men, one with blonde hair and one with brown, both humourless and silent.

"How was your flight?" Bradley held his arms out for Hisashi, but his smile seemed forced, his manner subdued.

"What's wrong? Where's Emmy?" On numerous phone calls in the last week, she'd given me the confidence I could make this move, and now she wasn't here?

"There was a small incident at the airport, and she had to stay behind."

"What incident? Is she coming later?"

He waved his free hand as Hisashi reached for the diamond earring he seemed so fond of. "Nothing you need to worry about, but I'm afraid it's just you and me, doll. And this little one, of course." Bradley ducked his head to the side as I unpeeled Hisashi's fingers from his earlobe.

His words made light of the situation, but his demeanour told me it was more serious than he let on. A chill ran through me as I remembered Hisashi's father's last words: "Don't worry, *querida*. Soon it will just be you and me."

Only it wasn't. He left and he never came back.

I wanted to ask more questions but Bradley was already marching ahead towards the exit. I hurried to catch up as the brown-haired man grabbed my suitcase.

"Where are we staying?" I asked, ducking my head to climb into a waiting SUV. I'd lined up apartments to look at, but Emmy said she'd sort out a hotel room for me until I found somewhere.

"The Four Seasons. I've booked a suite with a couple of bedrooms."

"Thank you."

When we walked into the lobby, half the people turned to stare at our strange little group. A Japanese girl and a baby, a guy in pale purple skinny jeans and a Banksy print T-shirt, plus two suit-clad bodyguards—I could hardly blame them, but that didn't make their stares any easier to take. Hisashi chewed on his fingers then shrieked, and everyone else swung their eyes in our direction as well. I tried my best to settle him, but at only a year old, he didn't appreciate five-star luxury.

I kept my eyes fixed downwards as Bradley marched to the desk and checked us in, only looking up when we went into the penthouse. The two bodyguards took up residence on the couch while Bradley followed me into my bedroom.

"You okay?" he asked. "You've been even quieter than usual. I thought you'd be excited."

I sat down on the edge of the bed and shrugged. "Try terrified."

"Why?"

I'd never tried to put the fear into words before. "It's all so new. I've never had to look for a home before, or interview someone, or live alone. Well, I'll have Hisashi but you know what I mean."

If anything, having Hisashi with me made things worse. I had to be responsible for a whole other human being when I barely felt capable of looking after myself. In an attempt to stop myself from panicking, I'd spent the last week trying to be practical. I'd spent my evenings trawling through property rental websites and registered with a nanny agency. After Emmy background-checked the candidates for me, I was left with three possibles.

"You won't be on your own. I'm here to start with, and you'll have a team of bodyguards if you need help."

"That's another problem. How can I act normal with that pair following me around?" I nodded at the door where Robocop and Terminator stood side-by-side, glowering.

"I see your point. They are kind of tall. I'll get them swapped out for different ones."

"I didn't mean them specifically. I meant having any two men at my heels. It was the same in Japan. It drew everyone's attention." At first having bodyguards gave me a sense of security, but as the months wore on their constant presence made me feel on edge. I'd planned to speak to Emmy about it but now she wasn't here. "I want this to be a new start, one where I can forget my past, and I can't do that with a pair of goons next to me. Can't you ask them to leave?"

His look of horror told me what he thought of that suggestion. "Not my decision, I'm afraid."

"Then I'll have to ask Emmy."

"She's not contactable right now. Maybe in a day or two." He opened the minibar and pulled out a bottle of orange juice. "Drink?"

I shook my head, trying to hide my frustration at his change of subject. This was my life, not his, and not Emmy's. Why was it so much to ask to live it as I pleased?

"Why don't you unpack?" Bradley asked. "And where are those apartment brochures?"

"It's too big," I said, as the realtor showed us round the first of the four potential homes we were due to see. "It looked much smaller on the internet."

Emmy found the apartment in Tokyo, and it had been surprisingly cheap. Although it was far larger than we needed, I'd fallen in love with the view and when my parents came to see it, their awed faces had me signing the purchase contract. But in Boston, there was no need for me to live on such a grand scale.

Bradley didn't share my sentiments. "I don't think it's big enough. I mean, it's only got three bedrooms."

"That's plenty."

He looked at me as if I'd suggested pink wasn't the best colour or chocolate was an unnecessary indulgence and ticked points off on his fingers. "One, Hisashi will want his own room before you've finished college. Two, you need somewhere for the nanny to sleep. Three, your family will come and stay." He scratched his chin. "You need at least five."

"Hisashi can share with me if my family all come at once, and who said the nanny would be living here?" True, I didn't like being on my own, but I valued my privacy too much to share my home with a stranger.

"Well, I just assumed... Why wouldn't you want her to stay? It'll be easier for everyone."

"I don't want a live-in nanny."

"I really think..."

"I appreciate you coming to help, honestly I do, but this is my fresh start. I need to learn to stand on my own two feet and cope by myself. That means a live-out nanny and no bodyguards."

"I'm not sure..."

"I am. Look, if I can't speak to Emmy, then you'll need to. No more shadows."

"I'll see what I can do, but she won't be happy."

I'd spent my whole damn life trying to make other people happy. "I'm sorry about that, but she'll have to live with it."

Apartment two was a bust, I knew it as soon as I heard the music blaring into the hallway from the place next door. Still, we politely looked around before we moved onto the next viewing, a three-storey block in a small complex.

"I'm not sure about this one, either," I whispered as we waited for the elevator. "It seems more like a retirement home."

Bradley wrinkled his nose. "The hallway smells of mothballs."

An old lady shuffled past, leaning on a walking frame, and scowled when she saw Hisashi. Their feelings appeared mutual, because he started to cry, and no amount of cuddles would placate him.

"Bad vibes," Bradley whispered.

Luckily the elevator dinged, and we practically ran on board. The realtor pasted on a smile as she eschewed the benefits of the place, ignoring Hisashi's snuffles.

"So, I know there are a lot of seniors around, but that's actually great for security. They've even organised their own neighbourhood watch program" she said.

Wonderful, nosy neighbours keeping an eye on my every move. "Sounds great."

"What would they do? Club a burglar to death with their walking sticks?" Bradley muttered.

"Sorry, what was that?" the realtor asked.

"Nothing."

The apartment wasn't too bad inside. The windows looked out over the communal garden, and if you ignored the grab rails in the bathroom it was quite practical. Although one oddity aroused my curiosity.

"The place is rented furnished, but there's no bed in the master bedroom?"

"Ah, yes. The landlord, er, took it out," the lady said.

"Why?"

"It's okay, he'll buy a new one."

Bradley planted himself in front of her, and I caught a rare glimpse of the toughness he normally kept hidden. "Why'd he take the bed out?"

"Er, the previous occupant passed away in it. They didn't find him for a few days."

I was halfway through the door before she finished the sentence. "No. Just no."

"Let's hope the last apartment's good," I said to Bradley over dinner. We'd ordered room service and ended up with twice as much food as we could actually eat.

"At least it's bigger."

"And one of these candidates had better be suitable." I thumbed through the stack of résumés the agency sent over. My initial favourite got rejected by Emmy after she found out the woman got fired from a previous position for smacking the child under her care. Of the three left, one was young, just nineteen, but the other two were in their forties. Hopefully they had the experience I was looking for.

"Don't worry," he said, popping a maki roll into his mouth. "We've got almost three weeks left to get things sorted. It'll be fine."

He had to eat his words the next morning as we stood in apartment number four.

"What's that big crack in the wall?" I asked.

The realtor followed my gaze up to the ceiling and went a shade paler. "I'm not sure. I don't recall it being there last time I came."

Bradley took a step to the side. "If you stand at the right angle, you can see daylight through it."

I clutched Hisashi to me, visions of the apartment tumbling down around us flying through my mind. "I think we should leave now."

Even the agent didn't hesitate as we hurried for the door.

"So what now?" I asked when we got outside.

Bradley pointed at the building. "Look, the cracks

start at the ground and go all the way up."

Sure enough, they did. Ugly black lines traced up one side of the building. A shudder ran through me. "I'm not setting foot in there again, but now I'm out of options." I turned to the realtor. "Do you have anything else on your books?"

"Most of the cheaper properties have already been snapped up by students. You started your apartment-hunting a bit late."

Tell me something I didn't know. "So you've got nothing?"

"We did have one new place come onto the books this morning. It's a little bigger than you were looking for—five bedrooms—but it's available immediately."

I ignored Bradley's grin of triumph. "What's it like?"

"It's not far. How about we stop by on the way back to the office?"

"I guess it can't hurt."

Oh it could. I felt it right in my wallet the instant I crossed the threshold. "This place is beautiful."

The apartment was on the fourth floor out of four, which meant it had a roof terrace and a hot tub, although I'd have to keep the door securely locked with Hisashi around. One bedroom was even set up as a nursery, with a child gate in the doorway and covers over the electrical outlets.

The huge lounge had plenty of space for a piano, and the windows looked over a nearby park. For only the second time in my life, I fell in love.

"How much?" I whispered.

At first I thought I heard her reply wrong. "How can it be only fifty dollars a month more than the place with the cracks? It's twice as big."

She shrugged. "The lessor's after a quick deal. His job's taken him and his family abroad, and he doesn't want it sitting empty."

"When's he coming back?" The last thing I wanted was to get settled then have to vacate the place.

"Apparently it's a five-year contract. He's looking for a long-term tenant."

"I'll take it." I was as surprised as Bradley looked when the words left my mouth. Rarely did I make such impulsive decisions, but it seemed to get easier with practice.

The realtor's shoulders slumped, no doubt in relief that we wouldn't need to traipse around any more apartments. "I'll get the paperwork drawn up."

CHAPTER 6

IT TURNED OUT finding an apartment was the easy part. As the last nanny applicant left the room, I felt like slamming the door behind her.

"I know in an ideal world recycling absolutely everything would be lovely, but it's hardly practical." I'd cringed at the lecture she gave me when the room service waiter brought us paper napkins. Apparently unbleached linen was the only way to go.

"And where the hell does she plan to compost the nappies? You'll be living in an apartment for crying out loud," Bradley said.

The younger girl had been sweet but too inexperienced and the second lady scared me. At this rate I'd be playing the piano at school with Hisashi in a rocker next to me. "I'll try the agency again. Who knows, maybe they'll have another suggestion?"

Miracle of miracles, they did. "A new candidate registered with us yesterday, and she sounds like the sort of person you're looking for. Her references look great and she's experienced."

"Could you send the details over?"

The instant the email landed, Bradley started Blackwood off on a background check. By the next day, we knew Sofia Drake wasn't a serial killer and had spent the last three years working for a family in New

York.

"Why did you leave?" I asked her when we met the day after that, a Friday.

"My employer moved abroad, to India, and I didn't want to travel that far. The boy I was looking after was almost ten in any case, so he wouldn't have needed a nanny for much longer."

"Why did you decide to move to Boston?" Bradley asked. "Why not stay in New York?"

"I grew up here, and although I loved New York I missed the slower pace of life."

"So your family still lives here?"

"My dad and step-mom retired to Hawaii and my brother works in Atlanta, so it's just me now."

"What made you become a nanny?" I asked.

"My mom died in a car accident soon after my brother was born, so I helped bring him up. I tried working in an office after I finished high school, and when I needed extra cash I started babysitting in the evenings. Believe me, if I could cope with my brother, I can cope with anything." She rolled her eyes. "Anyway, I preferred babysitting to filing and decided to do it full-time."

At least she sounded real. Candidate number one tried to convince me she'd felt a calling to be a nanny since she came out the womb, only when Hisashi cried she didn't know how to comfort him.

An hour flew by, and it was only when Sofia excused herself to use the bathroom I realised how long we'd been chatting. Yes, chatting. I'd long since given up on my list of questions as we discussed the best design of buggy and how important music was to a child's development.

"What do you think?" I asked Bradley, while she was out of the room.

He grinned. "Not a recycled hemp blouse in sight."

Hisashi made the final decision. When I carried him into the seating area, he made a grab for Sofia's colourful necklace and wouldn't let go. She took it in her stride and laughed with him as he bounced around on her lap. When the time came for me to take him back, he burst into tears. It was good to know where I stood.

"How soon can you start?"

"Are you serious?"

"Too serious," Bradley cut in. "Get her to loosen up a bit, would you?"

Sofia laughed and looked at me, clearly unsure what to say.

"Don't worry," I said. "I promise I'll try to relax more."

If only I'd known what Boston had in store for me.

"Ready for your first day?" Sofia asked.

"Just about."

With help from Sofia, as well as Bradley, who'd been summoned back to Virginia a few days earlier, I had a habitable apartment, food in the fridge and a selection of clothes in the wardrobe. That was all I really needed for now.

Well, there was one rather significant item missing —the gaping space at the end of the living room spoke of that. Sofia saw me look in that direction and grimaced.

"How long now? Five weeks?"

"Four weeks and six days." I'd started a countdown in my head to the day my new piano arrived. I could have bought any old grand, but I had my heart set on a customised Fazioli F212. The waiting list for those was months long, and even Bradley couldn't convince them to build one faster.

"Well, don't you worry. Just stop at school and practice for as long as you need." She held up Hisashi's hand and helped him wave to me. "We've got plenty of snacks for our cartoon marathon."

When the bad news about the piano came, Bradley offered to provide a substitute for the month. But as he was trying to work out the logistics of craning the thing into the apartment, Sofia offered to watch Hisashi for a couple of extra hours in the evenings so I could use one of the practice rooms at school until the Fazioli arrived. That seemed the best temporary solution all round. I'd miss Hisashi terribly, but I kept telling myself it was only for a few weeks. I could cope with anything for a few weeks.

"Are you sure you don't mind staying?"

"The only thing waiting for me at home is Netflix."

"Why don't I practise for an hour, then we can get a takeaway and watch something here?"

She broke into a smile. "You know what? That sounds great. What kind of food do you want? I can put in the order."

I grinned back, a feeling I was only just getting used to. Smiles used to be few and far between for me. "That sounds perfect. You pick. I'll eat anything."

Life was starting to click into place. Emmy had even agreed to scale back on my protection detail. As long as

I took a Blackwood car to and from school and promised not to walk anywhere alone, she called off the guards. Yesterday I had my first trip in the park with just Sofia and Hisashi, and the number of stares I got diminished vastly.

As I travelled to school in the back of a black SUV, I kept my fingers crossed that the rest of the adventure would be as smooth.

CHAPTER 7

DESPITE THE HOLBORN Conservatory being a music school, I spent most of the first day talking. Or rather, avoiding talking. The teachers set up a series of ice-breakers for the old students as well as the new, and I tried to stay as quiet as possible without being out-and-out antisocial. When someone asked about my background, I could hardly explain I'd spent fifteen years living in the jungle, could I?

By the end of the day I was exhausted, but I needed to fit in some practice before I left. I'd skipped too many sessions in the last month and according to my timetable I had a private piano lesson tomorrow at nine. My new teacher wouldn't be impressed if I couldn't remember where middle C was.

"You need a hand?"

A sandy-haired guy strode towards me, smiling, as I studied the map given to all the newcomers. I recognised him from the introductions earlier, but I couldn't remember his name.

"Uh, that would be good. I'm not sure I've even got this the right way up, er..."

"Jude. Jude Radley. You're Akari, right?"

Great. Now I felt even worse for forgetting his name, although I recalled his accent. British, a little upper-class like Hugh Grant. "Yes, that's right."

He took the map out of my hands and rotated it ninety degrees. "Now, where are you trying to go?"

"I need to find a practice room."

"The closest ones are here." He pointed at a spot just down the corridor. "But I'd recommend the two on the first floor. The acoustics are better. You want me to show you where they are?"

"That would be very kind of you."

He set off along the hallway, pausing for me to catch up at the corner. His legs were far longer than mine. At five feet four, most men towered above me.

"We barely got a chance to speak earlier," he said as we waited for the elevator. "You're a piano major?"

"I've never learned to play anything else. How about you?"

"Strings. Cello mainly, but I also play double bass. I always thought piano would be tough, having to play on your own all the time. At least in an orchestra it doesn't show up so much if you make a mistake."

"I hate to make mistakes." Which was why I needed to practise.

He laughed cheerfully as we stepped into the elevator. "Avoiding them's impossible. I found life's much easier if I accept them and move on."

I wished it were that easy. When I was thirteen, Okasan told me not to go out alone, but I knew better. A need to buy the latest magazine led to kidnap, rape and imprisonment. How the hell did I move on from a mistake like that?

"I'd still rather get things right."

He laughed again then led me halfway along a wide corridor, stopping at a door on the right. "Here you go. Have fun." He backed away with a wink, leaving me alone with my thoughts and a Steinway grand.

As I settled down on the padded seat in my new school, in a new city, in a new country, the realisation struck me that I was looking forward to life, my new life, for the first time in two years.

There was only one thing missing. "Wish you were here, C," I whispered to the photo of Hisashi's father that I'd drawn out of my purse and placed on the edge of the piano.

Of course there was no answer, but when I looked out of the window at the twinkling stars, I fancied one of them shone a little brighter that night.

My fingers ached at the end of my first lesson in Boston. I'd thought Noumura-sensei had been a tough teacher, but Dr. Vasilyevich made him seem like a holiday rep.

"You are rushing through the middle. The music has to speak to your audience, and at the moment your playing says one-night stand rather than a love affair."

Never having experienced the former, I had to take his word for it as I raised my tired wrists to the keys once more. Four more run-throughs and he finally pronounced me done.

"You have a lot to learn, young lady," he said, as I pushed the stool back.

"I look forward to it." I tried to inject some enthusiasm into my voice, but the session left me drained.

And that was only the start. My jammed timetable scarcely left me time to breathe, and it wasn't just full of music, either. The fellows at Holborn believed in a rounded education, so after lunch I had a lecture on English literature followed by a health seminar. And all students were supposed to choose an option from yoga, Pilates or dance and stick with it. I decided I was least likely to make a fool of myself doing yoga, so I signed up for a class each Thursday afternoon. That would also mean buying more clothes—no skimpy vests for me. I'd need sporty long-sleeved tops and full-length yoga pants.

Between my applied music lessons, the aural training, keyboard studies, music theory and a sonata class, I could barely keep my eyes open on Friday evening. And next Monday, I'd be assigned to a three-piece mixed ensemble and expected to practise for that as well.

Tempting though it was to stagger out to the car and go home, I turned instead towards the waiting piano. Only four weeks and one day left until my Fazioli arrived and I could play in the sanctuary of my apartment. Sofia had sent me a photo of her and Hisashi watching cartoons an hour ago, so at least somebody was having fun. I never realised following my dream would be such hard work, but the amount I'd learned in five long days surpassed a month of my solo lessons.

The corridors lay silent as I climbed the stairs to the first floor. The lift would have been faster, but I hadn't been getting enough exercise lately. Maybe I should take a walk to the park during the weekend? Although I'd have to call Blackwood if I did, because if Emmy found I'd gone out without bodyguards I'd be in for a tongue-lashing, and I could hardly ask Sofia to come with me on her days off.

A faint green glow illuminated each light switch, and I flicked them on as I went. Maybe not so kind to the environment, but darkness gave me the creeps. For the first year I was held prisoner, my captors threw me into a dark cellar when they were done with me each day, and even now I couldn't bear the pitch black. Hisashi wasn't the only one with a nightlight in our little household.

But now I was safe. I just had to keep reminding myself of that fact.

In the practice room, I drew the sheet music I needed to learn from my bag and propped it up on the piano. While Vivaldi wasn't new to me, he'd never been one of my favourite composers, and after a couple of run-throughs my attention wandered, and I started to play a rock song I heard on the car radio that morning. Oh, what the hell, there was nobody else around, so I began singing, too. I could hold a tune, but my version of "Bohemian Rhapsody" wasn't a patch on Freddie Mercury's.

I'd got halfway through the second verse when a shadow flitted across the doorway. My fingers played on for a few bars of their own accord then stopped, frozen in mid-air. Who was out there? I paused, listening carefully, but there were no footsteps, no voices. Had I been imagining things?

A faint squeak sent a jolt of electricity down my spine. Someone *was* there. Or something. My brother used to read me horror stories when I was a little girl, and although I'd been careful not to show how scared I was, the child in me still believed in monsters under the bed.

Grabbing the nearest heavy object, which happened to be a slender glass vase from a nearby side-table, I crept over to the open door. I hefted my makeshift weapon in my hands. Surely it couldn't be that valuable?

I held my breath as I peered around the edge of the doorframe then...relaxed. At the far end of the corridor, a janitor pushed a soft broom back and forth, and another soft squeak escaped from his rubber-soled shoes.

He looked up as I stared at him, then his gaze dropped to the vase I held. "Is everything all right, miss?"

I struggled to work out his age as half his face was hidden by a thick beard, but he sounded younger than I'd first assumed. "Yes, fine. You just took me by surprise. I thought I was on my own."

He stepped forward, and as he passed under a light I got a better look at him. Light brown hair curled over the collar of a pair of grey overalls, reaching his shoulders. When he got within touching distance, I read the name embroidered on the pocket. Lincoln. The material itself stretched over a muscular chest, but that wasn't what made my breath hitch as I looked up. His eyes drew me in, two dark brown pools that whispered of more secrets than a Mexican cenote. I struggled to tear my gaze away, only able to breathe again when my eyes fixed on the tiled floor. The floor was safe. The floor didn't know what I was thinking.

"I drew the late shift today. I'll try not to disturb you," he said, his voice steady.

"You weren't. I was just...I'm not used to being alone." Why did I tell him that? I couldn't even admit my insecurities to my own family.

"We all get jumpy sometimes." He shifted his broom to the other hand and made to move past me. "Nice music, by the way."

"You're a fan of Vivaldi?"

He threw me a glance over his shoulder. "I was talking about Queen."

CHAPTER 8

ON MONDAY WHEN I saw the shadow in the hallway I
didn't panic. The vase would live to see another day. A
second later, Lincoln popped his head around the door.
"I'm outside again. Didn't want to scare you."

"I wasn't..." I started indignantly then trailed off.
Who was I kidding? Nobody carried a vase around for
fun. "Thanks."

He disappeared, and I tried to put his face out of
my mind as I started to play my part of Schubert's
Piano Trio No. 1. I'd been allocated into an ensemble
that morning, thankfully with Jude on cello, so at least
I had a friendly face with me. I'd been sitting next to
him when the groups were announced.

"Now you'll be able to see how many cock-ups I
make," he whispered, earning a dirty look from the
professor.

I half-smiled in return, more worried about my own
inadequacies showing through. When we'd introduced
ourselves to our peers last week, I was one of only three
students who'd never performed in public, and the
thought of freezing up on stage terrified me.

The professor read out the next name, "Brigitte du
Champ on violin," and a red-haired girl on the far side
of the room sighed.

Jude echoed her sentiments. "Don't worry, love, we

don't want you either."

I hated to be quick to judge, but I couldn't avoid the rumours already flying about her. She'd chosen to live on campus and so far she'd insisted on moving rooms because she didn't like the view, berated the cleaning staff for a lack of clean towels, and accused the chef of xenophobia because the menus in the cafeteria were only available in English.

And when we started our first rehearsal, it turned out I'd been right to worry. Despite Jude's crack about making mistakes, he played his cello beautifully, and it was me who managed to mess things up. Three times I got my fingers muddled so much we had to start over, and Brigitte made her feelings on the subject quite clear.

"This is supposed to be a school for the gifted. I've seen better pianists in bars."

"And I've seen chimps with better manners," Jude retorted, but I held up a hand to quiet him. I didn't want to cause an argument and besides, Brigitte was right. I needed to do better.

And that was why I played until my fingers seized up on that Friday evening. By the time I staggered out at ten, I could barely move my arms. Lincoln was the only person still around when I left. He gave me a little wave as I crossed the lobby, grateful to be heading for the car at last.

"She's awful!" I said to Sofia as I hastily swallowed a slice of toast the following Tuesday. "How can one person be so spiteful?"

After yesterday's ensemble session, where Brigitte suggested I faked my school audition video, and lunch, where she'd driven one of my classmates to tears with barbs about her weight, I wanted to take Brigitte's perfectly buffed nails and gouge her eyes out with them. I'd stayed silent on the subject, but that morning over breakfast I couldn't bite my tongue any longer.

"Just focus on yourself. Karma will get her in the end."

"'In the end' won't be soon enough. Our first recital's in two weeks, and every time I step into the same room as her she makes me break out in a cold sweat."

Hisashi laughed as Sofia fed him a spoonful of mushed up banana, then she straightened up. "We should pray karma gets her act together then, shouldn't we?"

After I kissed Hisashi goodbye, I muttered a quiet plea skywards as I hurried down to the parking garage. My usual driver was waiting for me, and I reluctantly climbed into the backseat.

"Good morning, ma'am."

"Please, call me Akari." I'd asked him twenty times. "And good morning, Clint."

Only I'd lied about it being good. Every day I spent at school, I missed Hisashi more and more. Deep inside, I was starting to wonder whether I'd made a terrible mistake coming to Boston. True, the instruction was second to none, but without my family around I felt lonelier than ever. If it wasn't for Sofia's down-to-earth attitude and ready smiles, I'd have packed up and gone home.

"Ready for another day in the fun factory?" Jude

asked when I plopped onto the seat beside him in our music theory class. "I brought you a coffee. Figured you'd need it with the hours you've been practising."

"Thanks." I took a sip gratefully. "Caramel syrup— perfect." I'd discovered the joys of flavoured coffee when I moved to Virginia with Emmy. She was somewhat of a coffee connoisseur.

"And cream." He rummaged in his rucksack. "And cookies."

Brigitte strode past, pausing only to scowl at the bag of snacks. "You won't fit into your dresses if you eat all those."

"Ignore her," Jude whispered. "She's just jealous."

But I couldn't. I'd had a baby, and I still carried proof of that on my hips and stomach. Stretch marks didn't lie, and although I'd lost most of the baby weight through running around after Hisashi, I couldn't deny my clothes were a little snugger than they should be. "I'd better pass."

He shrugged, broke one in half and popped a piece into his mouth. "Oh well, more for me."

I felt the first tickle of a cold at the back of my throat on Wednesday, and my constant sneezing earned a series of glares from Brigitte.

"Do you need to go home?" asked the doctor teaching our health class.

I gritted my teeth and shook my head. "I'll be fine."

But I was still battling on Thursday morning. Jude flopped back into the seat beside me and handed me a bottle of orange juice.

"Thought you could use this rather than coffee. You know, vitamin C and all that?"

"Thanks," I whispered.

My throat felt like someone had gone at it with sandpaper, but that wasn't my only problem as my muffled hearing caused embarrassment in our ear training class. The notes all started to sound the same, and when it came to singing music from the page, my voice came out as a croak. Brigitte performed beautifully, of course, then rolled her eyes when the girl next to me took her turn. Yoga wasn't much better, but miraculously Brigitte was nowhere to be seen. Probably she'd gone back to her coffin to sleep.

With only a week to go until my first public performance, I headed to the practice room as soon as I'd unbent myself from downward facing dog. My back ached as I settled onto the stool, and I rummaged in my bag for an aspirin. Who said exercise was a good idea?

Schubert grated on my ears as I began to play. I'd once loved that piece, but each time I struck a key, all I could see was Brigitte's smug face as she hit every note perfectly on her violin. Over and over again I played the bloody arrangement, over and over... And eventually it sounded like music again. The practice room took on new life, no longer the same box I'd been sitting in for so many evenings. Now it filled with a greater presence, one of warmth, love even. I took my eyes off the music and turned my head. Someone was watching me from the doorway.

No, not someone. Hisashi's father. One step at a time he came closer, and I wanted to run to him, to throw myself into his arms and tell him how much I loved him. How much I'd missed him. Only I was frozen to the seat, my fingers playing of their own accord no matter how hard I willed them to stop. Why couldn't I move? When he got close, the one man I'd ever loved paused and reached out, touching not my heart but my shoulder.

"Miss?"

I reached up, closing my hand over his, finding his skin warm to the touch. But why was my face so cold?

"Miss?"

The voice was wrong. Why was he speaking with an American accent rather than his usual sexy Spanish?

"Miss?"

I woke with a start, groaning when I realised I'd fallen asleep on the piano. Oh hell, I'd drooled on the keys. I tried to wipe up the mess with my sleeve, putting off the moment when I turned to face...

"Hi, Lincoln."

"Long day?"

Just act natural, like waking up with three black keys and four white ones imprinted on your cheek was perfectly normal. "You don't know the half of it."

He leaned on the piano, and I resisted the urge to tell him off. "I know you practice longer than anybody else here."

"Because I need to. I'm supposed to be playing in an ensemble next week with a girl who makes Donald Trump look modest."

Why did I tell him that? I shouldn't burden others with my problems.

"You mean Brigitte?"

"You know her?"

"You're not the only person she's made an impression on since she arrived here. The catering staff have been queueing up to spit in her dinner and housekeeping are responsible for the sudden glut of spiders in her room. You didn't hear the news, then?"

"No, what news?"

"Brigitte has left the building."

"What, for today?"

"No, permanently?"

My eyes went wide. "You're kidding. What? Why?"

He chuckled, the sound deep and hearty. "The dean found out about a little movie she made in France and wasn't too thrilled. He doesn't like students bringing the school into disrepute."

"What kind of movie?"

"She tried to write it off as expressing herself through art, the dean's PA said, but given that it starred her, three men and no clothes, the dean didn't buy it."

I almost choked on my own tongue. "Porn?" I whispered. "She made a porn film?"

"Indeed she did, and her acting skills are no better than her interpersonal ones."

"You've seen it?"

"The support staff held their own showing at lunchtime. Chef even made popcorn."

"Oh, I wish I'd been there." I felt my cheeks turn red. "No, no! Forget I said that. I don't ever want to watch her doing...that."

He laughed louder that time, and I made the mistake of looking at his eyes. Such a deep brown, and up close tonight I saw the flecks of gold rippling around the edge of the irises. They were kind eyes, the fine lines spreading from the corners hinting at past laughter.

"I don't blame you. It was kind of interesting, but in

the same way a presidential debate is interesting. Everyone faking for the camera while they try to shove it up each other's ass, and the only reason anyone watches is because there's nothing better on the other channels."

"I can't believe it." I still struggled to accept the news. Was he joking? Had she really gone? "I've never been that lucky."

He pushed away from the piano. "Maybe that's changing."

As I watched him walk away, I mused over his words. Could he be right?

Friday morning came, and the empty seat in the seminar room told me Lincoln hadn't been lying. Whispers flew around my fellow students, but none of them seemed to have been privy to the gossip. I certainly wasn't about to spread it.

Dr. Vasilyevich arrived a little late with an unfamiliar face in tow. The entire class went silent as the door clicked closed behind them. It hadn't taken long for everyone to realise that Dr. Vasilyevich was not a man to be messed with.

I tried to study the newcomer without being obvious—easier said than done as he was doing the same, gazing around the class. He was the same height as Jude but a little skinnier, probably because Jude never stopped eating. Beside me, Jude didn't seem so curious about our new classmate as he snuck a gummy bear into his mouth and chewed. I shook my head as he raised an eyebrow in my direction. Dr. Vasilyevich didn't tolerate snacking.

"I would like to introduce a new pupil. Jansen has transferred across from the Conservatorium van Amsterdam, and I want you all to join me in welcoming him to Holborn."

A smattering of applause sounded from around the room, and I joined in as Jansen took Brigitte's chair. Would he be an improvement on its previous occupant?

"Jansen plays the violin, so as Brigitte has unfortunately had to leave us, he will take her place in the recital next week," Dr. Vasilyevich announced.

I figured I was about to find out.

CHAPTER 9

"WHAT'S YOUR BACKGROUND, Jansen?" Jude asked, as we traipsed to our allocated practice room.

"I picked up my sister's violin when I was five and started to copy her. When I proved my skills my parents agreed to pay for lessons."

"And you used to live in Holland?"

"Yes, we moved from Nijmegen to Amsterdam when I was eleven."

"So what made you leave? Why come here rather than stay at the Conservatorium?"

"My father's senior vice president of a marketing consultancy and the company transferred him over here on a two-year contract. I could have stayed behind but Holborn has a reputation for being the best, and I didn't want to pass up the opportunity. How about you?"

Jude answered first. "Similar start. I played the cello at school in England to avoid gym class, and when I didn't burst my parents' eardrums they forked out for extra tuition. But I moved here to get away from my parents, not stick with them." He paused and wrinkled his nose. "Although it's kind of quiet on campus. I'm gonna start heading out in the evenings to find out what the rest of Boston has to offer, if you want to join me?"

"I've never been a fan of nightclubs. I prefer my music classical. And you, Akari? Should I call you Akari? Or do you shorten it?"

In my sheltered life, I'd never met a Dutch person before. Was Jansen's abrasive tone typical of the region, or down to his manner? "Akari's fine. I started playing the piano when I was young, but I had a break for a few years so I'm not as advanced as the others here."

"Why would you have a break?" He sounded shocked at the concept. "Either music's in your blood or it isn't."

"Circumstances beyond my control. Now I'm able to play again, I have no intention of stopping." I had no intention of telling a stranger about the reasons, either. "How do you want to start the Schubert? Should we play individually first?"

I relaxed a little when I found Jansen's playing to be competent. He lacked Brigitte's flair, but he got the notes right and his tempo was spot on. Maybe we'd get through next week's performance after all? With that in mind, we played for the rest of the morning, until our grumbling stomachs reminded us they needed food.

"What's the cafeteria like?" Jansen asked me, as Jude led the way downstairs.

"Not bad. I mean, considering it's free." Holborn provided meals for each student as part of our scholarship although I preferred to eat my dinner at home with Sofia. Having crowds of people around me while I dined reminded me of meals in Colombia, where I ate at a communal table or I didn't eat at all.

I helped myself to a plate from the buffet and found a table in a quiet corner, but before I could take a mouthful, Jansen squashed onto the bench next to me and Jude sat down opposite.

"The food in Amsterdam was better." Jansen picked at his hamburger before covering it in ketchup.

"Nothing beats fries," said Jude.

Jansen shuffled a little closer, until his thigh touched mine. With the wall in the way, there was nowhere for me to go. The forkful of pasta I'd just swallowed stuck in my throat as he fixed his eyes on me.

"You like the spaghetti?"

"It's okay."

"It's overcooked." His tone made it clear he didn't believe me.

"I'm just not all that hungry."

"How about I take you somewhere that serves better food after class?" He shuffled a little closer as he peered at the mess I'd made on my plate.

I shook my head as I shrank back in my seat, his touch bringing back memories I'd locked away since last year. While I avoided physical contact, I could keep them there. Emmy had made it easy for me up until now—she'd ordered every man in her employ never to lay a finger on me, and none of them would dare to disobey. The only people whose touch didn't make me recoil were Emmy herself and her husband—not even my own family knew the full extent of my scars.

"Why not? You have to eat, and we can talk about our musical talents."

"I can't."

Nor could I stand being next to him for a moment longer. Leaving my lunch behind, I scrambled over the back of the seat as curious faces turned to stare. Jude called my name, but I ignored him. I didn't want to talk —not to him, not to anyone. A hundred eyes followed me as I fled towards the exit, speeding into a run as I got closer to freedom, then wincing as my wrist hit the door at an awkward angle. Only when I reached the safety of a locked toilet stall did I pause for breath.

What had I done?

I'd embarrassed myself in front of my classmates and overreacted at Jansen's innocent gesture. After all, he'd only offered to take me for some nicer food. A tear escaped down my cheek as I replayed the scene in my mind. They probably thought I was crazy, and I couldn't blame them. I'd often thought the same myself.

My fingers flew over the keys as I hammered out Scriabin's Black Mass Sonata that evening, ignoring the pain in my wrist. If I concentrated hard enough on the music, I almost forgot the whispers that had flown around as I walked into class earlier that afternoon. Jude looked away from me, while Jansen simply stared. I'd slunk away to the back corner of the lecture theatre and stayed there until the literature seminar ended.

Now it was just me, a piano, and my wayward thoughts. I used to wish for a magic switch to erase the horrors of Colombia which haunted my mind, but I stopped doing that a couple of years back when I fell in love with Hisashi's father. I'd keep the bad memories as long as he walked among them, but I needed to learn to control them better, something I'd thought would get easier with time but had so far proved me wrong.

I paused to gently work my wrist back and forth, trying to ease the pain. Yes, I knew I should rest, but playing was the only way to get rid of the fear and agony inside. If only...

"Late again?" A voice came from the doorway, making me jump. Lincoln walked towards me, tentatively covering the distance between the door and the piano.

I shrugged, and that sent another burst of pain shooting through my wrist.

"What's wrong?" he asked.

"Nothing."

"You don't screw your face up like that over nothing." He took another step, and I shuffled away a couple of inches, hoping he wouldn't notice. Thankfully, he didn't come any closer. "What happened to your wrist? It's swollen."

"An argument with a door. It'll be fine."

"Not if you keep thumping the keys like that, it won't." He drew a small package from his pocket and placed it on top of the piano. "I brought this for you. I thought you might be hungry after you left your lunch. You eat while I find you some ice."

Before I got a chance to protest, he'd gone. I snatched the greaseproof paper-wrapped object from the lacquered surface, checking it hadn't left a mark. The realisation he'd seen my lunchtime antics made my stomach sink. I didn't know why that mattered to me, but it did.

A whiff of chocolate fought with the sick feeling in the pit of my stomach, but hunger pangs won out, and I unwrapped Lincoln's offering. A chocolate brownie. I couldn't resist breaking off a piece and popping it in my mouth, then another.

"Didn't think you'd be able to say no."

I looked up to find he'd returned, complete with an armful of medical supplies and a smile.

"It's really good." I wiped a crumb from the corner of my mouth and tried to return the sentiment.

"Finish it off then I'll strap up your wrist. You should get it checked at the hospital."

I dropped the brownie and clutched my arm to my chest. My heart beat faster, the vibrations making my wrist throb more. "No, I'll be fine."

He dropped to his knees beside me. "What's wrong?"

That action caused my breath to hitch, because it reminded me of the time another man had done the same. I gulped in air, willing myself to keep control. "I don't like people touching me. That's all. If you leave the ice, I'll wrap it myself."

His frown deepened. "You ever tried doing that one-handed?"

A tear escaped, running down my face and plopping onto the remains of the brownie. "No."

"Hold your wrist out, and I'll put the bandage on. I promise I won't touch you, just the dressing."

"Are you sure?"

He smiled with his mouth but not his eyes. They remained dark, full of sorrow. "Trust me."

Trust him? I didn't know more than his name, and for me, trust took a lot more than that. But even so, something about his quiet manner told me he'd do as he said.

My hand shook as I held it out in front of me, and I couldn't help closing my eyes as he reached out. A plastic wrapper crinkled, and I felt him remove the silver cuff I wore, one of a pair. His sharp intake of breath told me the moment he saw what it covered.

"What the...?" his voice trailed off, but I didn't answer.

I couldn't. Words deserted me as he bandaged up the mess on my wrist, the same way Hisashi's father did four years ago when he found me in the basement with the stubby paring knife still in my hand.

As Lincoln worked, I remembered that day, the one that changed my life. It started off as any other day in hell did, with me waking at five to prepare breakfast for the bastards who'd held me captive for the last twelve years. Twelve years spent isolated in the jungle with the only way in or out by helicopter or a long journey along a rutted track. I'd tried to escape several times, and I still bore the bite marks from the dogs they'd sent after me. The last time, my leg ballooned up to the size of a watermelon, and I thought I'd die, until another of the servants packed my wounds with a paste she'd boiled up from leaves and the agony gradually subsided.

After that, I stayed put. With the choice of living uncomfortably or dying painfully, staying alive just squeaked it. Besides, as I grew older, life became more bearable, or maybe my senses became more dulled to the horrors. When I'd first been taken there, at thirteen, the novelty of a young foreign girl meant rape had been a daily occurrence. In my mid-twenties, I was more likely to get beaten for not cleaning well enough, or burning dinner, and out of the two I preferred the fists.

Until he came. The new guard, taller than the rest with a gold tooth prominent between his thin lips. He watched me for days, sending shivers through me every time I felt his eyes on my back. It was only a matter of time before he came for me, I knew that, and at the time I thought the waiting was almost more unbearable than the act itself would be. I'd been wrong.

He'd fucked my face, my vagina and then my ass, before forcing his gun barrel inside me in a final act of humiliation. As he twisted it round, cutting me with the iron sights, I'd never forget the look of malice in his eyes.

"Maybe I should pull the trigger," he whispered.

I lay there, helpless, my hands bound behind me. "Do it," I croaked back. "Do it."

But he didn't. His laugh flayed me as he pulled the gun out and did up his pants. "Too much mess. Besides, who would I have fun with for the rest of my stay here?"

That was the night I tried to kill myself, but I couldn't even get that right. I should have cut parallel with my arm rather than across it. Hisashi's father found me semi-conscious and carried me to his apartment, set aside at the opposite end of the hacienda to the rest of his family.

"Who did this?" he asked, still on his knees after he'd bound my wrists up and made me drink a gallon of water to rehydrate myself.

"I did."

"You might have held the knife, but you were not the cause."

"What does it matter? If it wasn't him, it would be one of the others."

His eyes, already so dark, turned black. "Give me his name." At six and a half feet tall, he towered over me, but the anger in his tone wasn't aimed in my direction.

"Ignacio," I whispered.

The second the name left my lips, he turned and strode off, leaving me alone in a place normally off limits to all the staff. His home contained little in the way of personal effects, the walls as blank as the persona he projected. I made it as far as the bedroom before weakness overcame me, and I collapsed on his bed, darkness overtaking my mind and my body.

A slamming door jerked me awake. How much time had passed? I looked around for a clock, but all I saw was his shadow silhouetted in the doorway. He glanced at me on his way across the room, pausing only to pull his shirt over his head and toss it in the waste bin in the corner. A metallic tang wafted towards me, and I fought to keep from gagging.

The light he flicked on in the en-suite bathroom bathed him in a soft glow, shoulders hunched as he rinsed the blood off a switchblade and returned it to his pocket. He didn't speak, but eventually I could stand the silence no longer.

"Are you okay?"

He stared past me, unspeaking, for so long I thought he wasn't going to answer, but then a single syllable left his lips. "No."

The thought that he'd injured himself for me sent me scrambling to get out of his bed. "I'll fetch the first aid kit," I rasped, but even before I'd finished the sentence dizziness overcame me, and I fell to the side.

"I'm not hurt."

"But you said..."

"I'm not okay. I am as much a prisoner here as

you."

"How? Your father owns the place."

"My father is a cold-hearted bastard. Now, you need to sleep."

I tried to get up again. "I'll go back to my room."

"No, stay." He dropped onto the other side of the bed and swung his legs up on the covers. "I won't touch you, if that's what you're worried about."

He lied.

I woke the next morning pressed against his chest, his arm slung across my waist. Feathery breaths puffed against my cheek, and when I raised my head I saw the frown lines he habitually wore less pronounced as he slumbered. I should have moved away, but I couldn't. Why? Because for the first time in twelve years, surrounded by his warmth, the darkness shrouding my heart lightened just a little.

The lights went out again when he died, and I thought my heart would forever be black. But as Lincoln strapped up my wrist, his eyes narrowed in concentration, a chink of light broke through the perpetual night.

CHAPTER 10

"YOU HAVE SOMEONE who picks you up, right?" Lincoln asked, as he tidied up the wrappings from the first aid supplies.

"How do you know?" Had he been watching me?

"I saw you getting into his car one night as I was leaving."

Oh. "Yes, I have a...friend who comes each evening."

"You need to get your friend to stop by the hospital on your way home tonight."

"I'll be fine."

"You don't know that." He crouched in front of me again, his eyes pleading. "You play so beautifully, don't risk that by not getting yourself checked out. Please."

When he put it like that, how could I say no? "Okay, I'll go."

"You promise?"

I nodded, and he smiled under his messy beard. "Good. You want me to walk you downstairs?"

My legs shook as I got up from the piano stool, and I clutched at the polished top with my good hand. Lincoln put out an arm, but stopped himself while it was a few inches away and slowly stepped backwards.

"Is that a yes?"

I nodded again, not trusting myself to speak.

Something about this man brought a lump to my throat, but I didn't understand what. Feelings were like that—they crept up at the most inopportune times and left me trying to puzzle out their meaning while the world carried on without me.

Lincoln held each door open for me while I trudged towards the exit, exhausted from the emotions of the day. Clint raised an eyebrow at my new companion as he got out the car to open the door for me. Then his eyes went to my wrist and widened.

"It's nothing," I said. "I just need to make a quick stop at the hospital on the way back."

"Of course, ma'am."

There was the "ma'am" again. It seemed the habit was ingrained. This time it was Lincoln's turn with the curious look, which I ignored as I slid into the backseat. Today was bad enough without trying to explain the bizarre life I led. Instead, I gave him a quick wave through the window as the car pulled off then settled back in the seat for the ride to the emergency room.

"Er, is there any chance you could not mention this to Emmy?" I asked.

"Sorry, ma'am. She's going to find out, one way or the other. Better to tell her now and get it over with."

I sighed as I settled back against the soft leather. "I'll call her in the morning."

With a sore wrist and now a bulky bandage, I gave up on the idea of practising at the weekend, and after an awkward phone call to Emmy, who already knew what happened, I spent my days off playing with Hisashi.

Most of the time I was blessed to have a good baby, but he'd also inherited his father's rebellious streak, and I had a hard time convincing him the cuddly cat Bradley mailed to the apartment on Thursday wasn't edible.

In the end, I called Blackwood and got them to send a couple of shadows around, and we spent an almost-pleasant Sunday afternoon in the cold yet sunny park before my good arm got tired from pushing the stroller. Sure, I could have asked one of the man-mountains to help, but requesting help never came easily to me. The therapist used fancy words and talked about my guilt complex, but I simply didn't want to take advantage of people.

By the time Monday morning rolled around, the swelling had subsided enough to take off the bandage, and I'd psyched myself up to face Jansen again.

Or at least, I thought I had.

"Where did you run off to on Friday?" he asked, as soon as we got into a practice room with Jude.

"I didn't feel well."

I looked away as I said it. Even though it wasn't entirely untrue, I struggled with the words. Hisashi's father said that was one of the things he loved about me, that I was the one person in that awful place who didn't lie, and my time there taught me that I valued the truth above all else.

"You should have said."

"Why? What would you have done?" asked Jude.

"I could have helped. If Akari felt sick she should have let us know so we could schedule our practices accordingly."

"If she was about to puke, I doubt she was thinking of that."

"We're supposed to be working as a team, here."

"Exactly, so show some sympathy."

Jude squared up to Jansen, and I stepped in to keep the peace. "I promise to keep you informed next time." I shuddered as the words left my mouth. I was hoping there wouldn't be a next time. "Why don't we play the Schubert now?"

Despite my hopes, next time arrived, and sooner than I could have anticipated. I'd barely sat down in front of the piano that evening when Jansen walked in carrying his violin, only this time Jude wasn't around to stick up for me.

Jansen laid his case on the table and unsnapped the clips that held it closed. "I thought we could practise together."

"I-I-I prefer to play alone."

Jansen lifted his violin from its case and cradled it in his lap as he perched on the edge of the table. "I also need to apologise, for being such a jerk this morning. It was rude of me to question you."

I shrugged. "It doesn't matter."

"It does to me. I don't want things to be awkward between us. After all, we'll be playing together the whole week and hopefully many more times in future."

Something about the way he said "playing" made my stomach clench and for a brief second I even wished Brigitte would come back. Then I came to my senses and forced myself to smile. Like it or not, I needed to remain on good terms with Jansen to pass this course, and no matter how unpersonable he might be there was no denying his musical ability.

"Of course. Would you mind if we just ran through a time or two so I can get home for dinner?"

"What's wrong with the cafeteria here? We can grab a sandwich then carry on."

"I thought you didn't like the cafeteria?"

"The food is unpalatable, yes, but we've lost too much time to waste more finding a restaurant."

"Someone is cooking for me."

His smile turned into a scowl. "This recital is important, and Jude's already demonstrated his lack of commitment. Do you want to fail as well?"

"No, but... Maybe we could practice again tomorrow evening?"

"We should play together every evening."

I almost told him about Hisashi, but it wasn't right to use my son as an excuse for a lack of work. The dean already questioned at my interview whether I could cope with my small family as well as my education, and I if I wanted to succeed I needed to learn to manage both.

"I'm still not feeling a hundred percent."

"Well, we'll have to make do with ninety. Luckily one of us has the skill and tenacity to make it at this place."

Skill and tenacity perhaps, but not compassion? What happened to compassion? Did it get muffled by his over-inflated ego? I almost snapped, but I bit my tongue and counted to ten instead. Maybe Jansen was right, albeit rude as well. I did need to ace this recital, and so I needed to practise.

"Okay, each evening until the recital." Even as I said it, thoughts of Hisashi made my breath hitch. "Shall we meet here?"

When he nodded, he displayed teeth a shade too white to be natural and smoothed his hair back. "Good. At least two of the three of us want to pass. I'll need to work on Jude tomorrow. Shall we start?"

I couldn't get my hands on the keys fast enough. I'd got through the first four bars before Jansen caught up, and I didn't pause until the end.

"You need to slow down," he said. "The piece was written to be played more smoothly."

"Sorry, I guess I'm just tired."

I willed myself to play steadily as we started from the beginning, but my fingers kept getting ahead of Jansen's steady beat. If I played like that on the day of the recital, my grade would be terrible, but my subconscious was convinced the faster I played, the quicker I could get away from a man whose dedication to the cause rivalled an Olympic athlete's.

"Better, but you're still rushing the middle part. Let's go again from the top of the second page."

My eyelids drooped and two of each note swam across my vision. "How about we call it a night? I promise to be more alert tomorrow."

"Quitters never win, Akari."

Surely even winners needed to eat and sleep at some point? I forced my mouth shut as it attempted a yawn of its own accord and tried to focus on the music.

"Good evening, don't mind me."

Jansen's eyes flashed with anger as Lincoln walked in pushing a cleaning cart.

"We're playing in here. Can't you clean someplace else?"

"This is the last room, I'm afraid. I'll make sure I

keep quiet." He took out a soft broom and started sweeping.

Jansen turned to me, still looking far from thrilled. "Fine, let's stop for today. I can't concentrate with him in here. We can do extra tomorrow."

"Great." Was a bout of food poisoning too much to hope for? Or maybe a short-lived virus?

With jerky movements, Jansen packed his violin back into its velvet-lined case then stomped out without so much as a goodbye. Not that I minded—as long as he was gone, I couldn't complain.

"Hope you didn't stop on my accord," Lincoln said.

"If I'd played much longer my fingers would have fallen off. I thought he'd never let me go home." The closer Lincoln got, the more my stomach fluttered, but not from worry this time. "You arrived at just the right time."

"Bit pushy, is he?" He leaned his broom against the cart and came over, stopping a few feet away.

"He just wants to get a good grade."

"Surely you'd score a better grade by getting some rest and eating properly. It's almost nine o'clock."

Oh heck, that last hour flew by so fast I'd hardly noticed it. I owed Sofia a huge apology. Although she said staying on in the evening wasn't a problem, I hated the thought of exhausting her as well. If Jansen kept this up, I'd have to consider employing a second nanny to do the evening shift. Mind you, even the idea of that filled me with sadness. Hisashi was my son. I should be the one looking after him, not a stranger, no matter how sweet she was.

"You're right. I need to get home."

"You want me to walk you out? You look like you're

about to nod off."

"I'll be okay. I don't want to keep you any later, either."

"It's no trouble."

"Honestly, I'll be all right. Although if you happen to interrupt again tomorrow I'll give you a medal."

He gave me a wink as I picked up my bag and started for the door. "Consider it done."

CHAPTER 11

"I PROMISE, IT'S only for this week," I said to Sofia as I shoved a banana into my bag to eat in the car.

She picked Hisashi up from the floor where he'd been arranging the sparkly animals Bradley bought him into piles. He howled for a second then giggled as she swung him around in the manner he loved. "Don't worry. He's such a good boy."

"I could hire an extra pair of hands to help you if you want?"

She waved me away. "Don't be silly. I've had far worse jobs than this. At least you don't expect me to unblock the toilet at two in the morning like my employer before last did."

"That really happened?"

She wrinkled her nose. "It was disgusting. They'd been out to a party and come back drunk. There was a hell of a mess."

The sight of the driver idling outside reminded me how late I was getting. "Well, I appreciate everything you're doing, but just let me know if it gets too much."

"Sure will." She held up Hisashi's hand. "Wave to Mommy, sweetie."

He giggled and waggled his fingers, and although it pleased me he was happy, it also saddened me that Sofia got to see him grow up more than I did.

I wasn't the only mother in that position, though. Thousands of parents the world over had to work while their children went to nursery. I was luckier than most because my son had one-on-one care and I got to do something I loved all day.

At least, that's what I kept telling myself, but as Jansen herded Jude and I into the practice room at five o'clock it was difficult to convince myself of the second part. Jude rolled his eyes at me as he took a seat and arranged his cello ready to play.

"From the top," Jansen instructed, focusing on Jude. "I hope you managed to do some sort of practice over the weekend."

"I performed this piece at a concert last year." Jude broke into a grin. "Plus I'm a natural genius."

Jansen didn't share his amusement. "Even the virtuosos need to practise. None of them became great musicians through singing karaoke in second-rate bars."

"Oh, lighten up, man, the karaoke was a hoot. Maybe you should join us next time, a few drinks might make you less uptight."

"Alcohol impedes my playing ability." He leaned closer to Jude. "Are you still hungover?"

Yes, I'd said I missed my child, but I had no desire to replace him with two more. "Will you two please stop arguing? The sooner we play, the sooner we can all go home."

At twenty-seven and twenty-six respectively, they should both know better, but they turned their backs on each other and marched to separate sides of the piano. Why did I feel like a referee?

As Jude glared at Jansen and picked up his bow,

the delicate notes of Mozart sounded, but rather than drifting in from an adjacent practice room, it came from my pocket.

"Excuse me a minute." Now it was my turn for the eye rolls.

I hurried into the corridor, suddenly worried. Mozart was the ring tone I'd assigned to Sofia and right now she should be settling down in front of the TV with Hisashi. What was wrong?

"Is everything okay?" I didn't bother with pleasantries.

"No. I mean, Hisashi's fine, but I've got a problem. Are you going to be late tonight?" I'd never heard Sofia anything but calm, but tonight her voice rose in panic.

"I'm still at school. What's wrong?"

"My landlord just called to say my apartment building's been condemned. I've got this evening to move my stuff and find somewhere else to live before he shuts the place up permanently."

"Condemned? What for?"

She gave a hollow laugh. "Oh, pretty much everything. Fire code violations, a problem with the wiring, cockroaches."

Good thing she wasn't there to catch the look of horror on my face. "That's awful. How did you put up with it?"

"I was saving up for something better, but as I was only going there to sleep it didn't matter too much."

"Have you got somewhere else to go?"

"I thought I'd find a motel then look for a new apartment at the weekend."

"Why don't you take one of my spare rooms?" I know I'd told Bradley I didn't want to live with a stranger, but Sofia was a friend now and after living with my family for a year, I had to admit to finding life in Boston a little lonely despite their daily phone calls.

"Are you serious?"

"They're only sitting empty. I'll come right home, and I can watch Hisashi while my driver takes you to collect your things."

"I don't know what to say, just thank you, thank you. I promise you'll barely notice I'm there."

As predicted, Jansen was less than impressed when I explained the situation. Jude simply shrugged and said, "These things happen," before packing his cello up faster than I'd imagined it to be possible and practically sprinting from the room.

"Same time tomorrow," Jansen yelled at his disappearing back.

"I can only apologise for this," I said as I sent a quick message to my driver asking him to come early.

"Sometimes I think I'm the only person round here who's actually serious about a career in music," he snapped, before he too left the room.

Were my motivations wrong? I played the piano because I loved it, not for the money. Many times the only way I could express how I felt was through music. The simple sounds combined to form an outlet for the emotions that built up inside me, which was perhaps why I tended towards the darker pieces Okasan hated to hear. Maybe in time I'd be able to play music I could smile about, but at the moment I needed to release the pain of all I'd experienced in life so far.

At this point, each evening I spent playing, first with Brigitte and now with Jansen, added to my frustrations rather than relieving them. I'd wanted my time at Holborn to represent a fresh start, but right now I was still bogged down in my past.

I passed Lincoln on my way to the exit, moving a floor polisher back and forth across the tiled floor of the atrium. He looked up as I approached then checked his watch and plucked out his headphones.

"Early finish today?"

"Something came up."

"Everything okay?"

I shrugged. "Honestly, I don't know."

"It have anything to do with the two guys who left before you? One was jogging with a cello, and the other looked like he was plotting a murder."

"Probably." The pick-up zone outside the glass doors was empty, and I figured my driver would be a few minutes so I sank down onto an ornamental stone bench to wait for him. "I can't work out what to do about them."

Lincoln abandoned his cleaning and sat on the other end of the bench, far enough away that I didn't feel the need to move. It was like he instinctively understood my boundaries and didn't push them.

"In what way? I've heard the dark-haired guy talk to other people, and if the music thing doesn't work out for him he could always get a job as a dictator."

I covered my mouth as I tried not to laugh. "I know school is important, but we've only been here for a few weeks, and he insists on practising our recital piece every evening until I can barely stay awake. Mind you, I can probably play the notes in my sleep now."

"What about the first guy?"

"He doesn't want to practise at all."

"And you're stuck in the middle, trying to keep both

of them happy?"

"Exactly." He'd put into words what I couldn't.

"And you're so busy thinking of them, you're miserable yourself."

"Yes. But I don't know how to change that. Jansen, the one with the dark hair, he doesn't listen to reason."

"Then don't try to reason with him. Set your boundaries and stick to them. It'll be uncomfortable at first, but it's better to do that than let him run you into the ground."

He spoke so much sense, yet the thought of standing up for myself against Jansen's withering glare and sharp tongue filled me with dread. "It's not always that easy," I whispered.

"Sometimes life is a journey through darkness, but as long as you have a spark inside, you can use it to light your way. Learn how to kindle it, and you'll burn bright."

Even though his smile was as kind as his words, a tear ran down my cheek. His eyes radiated warmth as he reached into his pocket and passed me a handkerchief.

"Thank you. I'll remember that." A movement outside caught my eye, and a black Mercedes glided to a halt in front of the doors. "I have to go now."

As I handed his handkerchief back, my fingertip touched his. The crackle of heat between us was unexpected, and I snatched my hand away, not through my usual revulsion but from surprise. Did he feel it too? His face registered nothing, just the steady calmness that seemed to be his default.

"I'll see you tomorrow, then." He tipped an imaginary hat. "Have a good evening, ma'am."

CHAPTER 12

SOFIA GOT UP early and went for a walk, but she got back before I needed to leave for school at eight.

"Are you back at your usual time?" she asked.

The grimace spread across my face before I could stop it. "Maybe even later if Jansen insists on making up for the time we lost yesterday."

"He sounds like a real piece of work. How long is the bit of music you're playing? Do you actually need to practice that much?"

"Only twelve minutes, and I know it already."

I'd memorised it by the third time I played it through. I'd been able to do that since I was a little girl. My first piano teacher refused to believe me at first, until she tested me by making me play a Bach piece I'd never laid eyes on before. Half an hour later, I knew it well enough to play in any key, and my tutor informed my parents I needed someone more experienced than her to further my musical education. Not that they could afford it, though.

"Just tell him you need to go home, then."

"That's what Lincoln said as well, but I tried that last week, and he wouldn't listen."

"Lincoln? Who's Lincoln?"

Oops. I hadn't wanted to mention him to anybody else, but it slipped out without me thinking. "Just the janitor at school. Jansen complained because he wanted to clean the practice room while we were still using it, but if he hadn't come in we'd probably have still been there at breakfast."

"Better keep your fingers crossed he does the same tonight."

Yes, I should, shouldn't I.

On our third attempt at Schubert that evening, Jude's lack of practice still showed. Not in a dramatic way, but he spent too much time concentrating on the mechanics of the piece rather than putting in the expression it needed.

"Again," Jansen ordered.

Jude looked at his watch. "No can do. I've got a date in half an hour."

For a second, I thought Jansen would self-combust. His face went a peculiar shade of pink and the growl that left his mouth hardly sounded human.

"We have to play in front of an audience in three days, and your date is more important?"

Jude shrugged. "She's hot."

Jansen grabbed Jude's wrist, but Jude had already mentioned to me that he went to the gym every morning and despite his penchant for eating junk food, it showed. He shook off Jansen like he was swatting away a pesky mosquito.

"Chill out, man. It's only the first semester, and I came to school to have fun, not work like a dog every bloody day."

Jansen seethed, I saw the fury in his eyes, but there

was nothing he could do as Jude packed his cello away and sauntered out the room.

Left alone with him, his spitting anger flecked my skin like red-hot barbs. I shrank backwards as he advanced, his mouth set in a hard line.

"Sit." He pointed at the piano stool.

The easy option would have been to do as he said, but when I thought back to Lincoln's words of the night before, I knew if I let him keep me there again, I'd always be under his thumb. "I-I-I need to get home as well."

"Later. We need to play first. The last section still needs work."

"But I have things to do at home."

"You don't understand. I refuse to fail this class, and Jude's already doing his best to sabotage the recital." He advanced, and I stepped backwards until the cool wood of the piano blocked my way. "Now, take your seat."

"Let her leave." A soft voice came from my right, and I looked up to see Lincoln in the doorway.

Jansen's lip curled up in a sneer as he turned his fury on him. "Get lost. This is none of your business."

Lincoln's stance stayed easy, relaxed, but a slight hardening of his body told me he wasn't impressed by Jansen's words. He walked towards us, hands loose at his sides, eyes fixed on Jansen.

"You made it my business when you tried to keep a woman here against her will."

Jansen's harsh laugh bit through the air. "Don't be ridiculous. Akari's happy to stay." He turned to me. "Right?"

What should I say? I was far from happy, but if I

said so Jansen would get even more upset, and I still had to work with him. He assumed silence to mean agreement and took a step towards Lincoln.

"See? Just remember what you're here to do—you clean, you don't talk to the students. Have some respect."

How dare he? "You're the one who needs to show some respect. Lincoln's a human being. How can you speak to him like that?"

"He's a janitor. You and I, we're different. We have the ability to make something of our lives." He turned his back on Lincoln. "Now, ignore the man and let's carry on."

"I need to go home."

"You need to practice. This school is the most competitive in the world, and if you want to succeed here you have to put the hours in." He gave me a little shove towards the stool, catching me by surprise, and I tripped over my foot before I caught the edge of the piano to save myself.

I glanced in Lincoln's direction, but he hadn't moved. He looked far calmer than I felt inside, although I noticed his hands balled up at his sides. Hisashi's father used to do the same thing in front of his own father and his brother. He'd once confided that it took all his effort to maintain his relaxed facade, when what he dreamed of doing was snapping their necks. What was going through Lincoln's mind?

"Don't touch her," he growled, taking a step forward.

"Or what? You'll stop me? I'll have you fired."

I willed him not to lay a finger on Jansen. Although I felt like punching the pig myself, I had no desire for

Lincoln to lose his job over me.

"It's okay," I whispered. "I can stay a bit longer."

Lincoln's hand reached out, eclipsing Jansen's triumphant grin. "You don't need to. You can come with me."

I stared at his fingers, holding steady a foot away from me, then looked at his eyes. They said what his mouth didn't: "I'll look after you."

The smugness on Jansen's face faltered when I didn't immediately laugh off the idea, and I longed to wipe it off completely. But to do so would mean touching Lincoln. That contact scared the hell out of me, but was it worse than spending the rest of the evening with Jansen?

No. No, it wasn't. I tried to wipe my sweaty palm on my trousers without anybody noticing then extended my hand towards Lincoln. It seemed to travel of its own accord, unconnected to my arm. The instant it touched Lincoln's own dry skin, his fingers curled around mine and a little of his strength transferred to me. I didn't look back at Jansen as Lincoln gathered up my bag with his other arm and led me from the room.

The instant we cleared the threshold, he went to drop my hand, but I clung on to what had become my lifeline.

"You okay?" he asked.

When I shook my head, he set off down the corridor towards the elevator. I looked back towards the practice room, half-expecting Jansen to follow, but there was no sign of him.

"Don't worry, he won't come after us tonight. He needs to regroup."

The elevator arrived, and Lincoln herded me inside.

As the doors closed, I sagged back against the mirrored wall, catching a glimpse of myself opposite. The stress of the last few weeks had taken their toll, and hollow eyes looked back at me from under a limp, too-long fringe.

"Regroup? What do you mean regroup?"

"He'll try to bully you down again, but you did well tonight. He fights with words, but you need to fight back with spirit."

Any spirit I had left me years ago, when I was kidnapped. Hisashi's father lent me his but when he died, it went with him. "I wish it was that easy."

"Could you change group?"

"Maybe. But Brigitte's already been excluded, and if I complain about Jansen and he gets in trouble then it might look as if I'm the problem rather than him."

"You had nothing to do with Brigitte leaving."

"I know, but everybody else might not see it that way."

Heat rose up my arm as he squeezed my hand. "Then we'll have to make sure you stand up for yourself. You want to wait downstairs with me until your ride gets here?"

I nodded, unable to speak as the corners of my eyes prickled. Kindness from strangers was a novelty that made me tear up, and I didn't want to look like an idiot in front of Lincoln.

The elevator arrived in the basement, a place where the low ceilings and lack of daylight made me shudder. Memories of being trapped in a cellar while fire raged through the building above flooded through me, and my pathetic whimper caused Lincoln to spin round, his eyes radiating concern.

"What's up?"

"I'm not so good in basements."

"We can go upstairs if you like."

And risk running into Jansen? "I'll be okay."

Breathe in and out. In and out. When I first got to America, Emmy showed me a series of breathing exercises, something she said helped her stay calm over the years in all manner of uncomfortable situations. Now I placed my hand on my stomach, feeling the movement as I breathed in on a count of five, paused and relaxed my shoulders, then exhaled slowly.

Lincoln opened the door to a small, messy office, the desk littered with scrawled notes, nails and screws. He dumped the remains of a sandwich into the bin then shoved a pile of papers off a tatty chair and helped me onto it. My legs dangled in the air, hardly surprising as he was almost a foot taller.

"Welcome to my palace," he said, giving me a lopsided smile before dragging over a toolbox and sitting down on it next to me.

The space may have lacked the opulent grandeur of the upstairs levels, but Lincoln's presence made it comfortable. "It's nice."

His laughter filled the space. "You're so damned polite."

"No, really it is."

"Then it's you who makes it that way. Did you call your friend to pick you up?"

What did he mean by that first part? Did he just pay me a compliment? If so, I didn't deserve it. All I'd done so far was put him in an awkward situation and take up his evening.

"Not yet, but I don't think I'll get a signal down

here."

He motioned at a phone on the desk. "Use that one. Do you want something to drink? Water?"

"Water would be good." The back of my throat had gone all scratchy, like sandpaper.

"I'll be right back." He rose to his feet with a grace that belied his size, leaving me with a view of his behind as he strode from the room. I couldn't tear my eyes away until the door clicked shut behind him. What was wrong with me?

My thoughts were still jumbled when he came back a couple of minutes later.

"Did you get hold of your friend?"

"Driver. He's only my driver." I had a concern that Lincoln might frown on me for that luxury, but I felt the need to clarify the relationship with the man who picked me up every evening. "He'll be here in ten minutes."

The condescending look I'd expected didn't come. "I'll stay here with you until he arrives. You did well this evening."

"If you hadn't been there, I'd have given in. Next time won't be so easy."

"Where's your phone?"

"What?"

"Your phone."

I fished it out of my pocket with my left hand and passed it over. Lincoln juggled it until it was the right way up then tapped away at the screen before handing it back.

"I'm nearly always here in the evenings. Now you've got my number, so you can message me if he behaves like an asshole again."

I almost hugged him but that was a step too far. I settled for a smile. "Thank you. You didn't need to do that this evening."

"I've watched him behave shittily since he got here, and not just with you. A girl in one of his other classes threatened to chop his junk off."

"She told you that?"

"In this uniform, I don't exist unless people want something, especially in a place like Holborn. I overheard her speaking to her friend as they walked past."

I knew how he felt. For years, I'd cooked and cleaned for people who didn't give me a second glance until they wanted a little fun in the evenings. I'd heard men confess to murder, talk about cheating on their wives, and plot out drug shipment routes. When I escaped I told everything I remembered to Emmy, and she'd passed it on to the authorities. Three months ago, she informed me the DEA seized over a million dollars' worth of cocaine headed for New York based on the information so at least my time in Colombia served some purpose.

"I'm glad you noticed me," I said softly.

"I don't pretend to know much about classical music, but I'd have to be deaf to miss the way you play." He chuckled. "I keep getting behind with the cleaning because I stop to listen."

"Really?"

"Really. You've got a magic touch on that piano." The phone rang, and he reached out for the receiver. "No, I'm the janitor... Yes, she's here. I'll bring her up."

He put the phone down and smiled. "Your driver's outside."

So soon? Ten minutes had flown by as I sipped water and listened to Lincoln's deep baritone. He stood, and this time when he held out his hand I didn't hesitate. He said I had a magic touch, but as his fingers wrapped around mine I had to disagree. It was he who held the power.

CHAPTER 13

THE BLACK SUV glided smoothly through the dusk, taking me back to Hisashi. Usually on the ride home, all I thought of was seeing my son but tonight the episode with Jansen, and indeed the aftermath, weighed heavy on my mind.

"Is everything okay, ma'am?" Clint's eyes watched me in the rear-view mirror.

"Yes, fine."

"I was a little surprised when a gentleman answered the phone."

I avoided telling him what happened at practice, because Emmy would hear about it before I got back to school the next day, and Jude and Jansen would most probably find themselves in the dean's office. And like I told Lincoln, I didn't want to get branded a troublemaker.

"Oh, I got done a little early so we were just chatting before I left. I was playing Schubert, and he likes to listen when he's finished work."

"He said he was the janitor?"

"Yes, I see him cleaning most evenings."

We lapsed into silence for the rest of the ride, and thankfully traffic was light. When I arrived home, Sofia and Hisashi were playing on a multi-coloured mat spread out in the living room, although Hisashi was laughing rather than matching up the shapes like he was supposed to. They both looked surprised when I walked in the door.

"I wasn't expecting you home so early. I haven't even started dinner yet."

"It's a surprise to me too."

"Did something happen?"

I'd never had a girlfriend I could confide in before, but I needed to talk to someone about the mess at school, and besides, Sofia deserved to know because it affected her as well. "Why don't we order a pizza and I'll tell you about it?"

"Sounds good to me. You go and change, and I'll get Hisashi's dinner ready so you can spend some time with him while we wait for the food to arrive."

What would I do without her? I hoped I'd never have to find out.

Feeding Hisashi took longer than usual because tonight he decided he hated carrots. Why today, of all days? I tried to get the spoon in his mouth once more, but he turned his head away.

"Please, little one. They're good for you."

He glared at me like carrots were poisonous. So tiny, yet he'd mastered the look perfectly.

"Your daddy loved carrots."

Even that didn't work. I was close to tears when Sofia gently took the spoon out of my hand. The frustrations of an awful week were catching up with me.

"How about I finish feeding him? I've got some melon slices if he won't eat carrots today. We can try the carrots again tomorrow."

"It should be me. I should be helping him with his

dinner."

"You've had a long day, and not a good one by the sounds of it. Why don't you order our dinner instead?"

Feeling utterly inadequate, I did as she suggested and ordered the pizza. Every day, I felt more homesick, and every hour I questioned what I was doing in Boston. Face it, I wasn't cut out for this world.

I slumped on a chair as Sofia did what I couldn't and convinced my son he loved carrots. Even though she was helping, the bond they'd so obviously formed made me feel worse than ever.

"I'll put him to bed," I said, once he'd finished the last spoonful.

"Are you sure? I don't mind."

"No, I'll do it."

Was Hisashi a baby or an octopus? I could have sworn on the latter as I changed his diaper then attempted to get him into his pyjamas. Arms and legs flailed everywhere, but I finally got him dressed. Even the simplest of chores seemed like insurmountable problems these days. And then he gave me another challenge.

"Corn," he wailed from his crib as I snuck out of the room.

I scurried back and tried to quiet him with a cuddly dog. The tatty toy was his favourite, but today it only made him screech.

"Cooooooorn." He pointed at the door.

"Corn? Why do you want corn? You already ate carrots."

At times like this I missed my mother and her advice more than ever. This child-rearing thing was so much harder than I imagined. Hisashi's cries got louder as I tried a furry dragon then a fish.

Sofia poked her head around the door. "Everything okay?"

"He wants corn. Do we have any corn?"

"He means the unicorn Bradley sent him. Hang on, I'll find it."

And she was right. The second Hisashi got his tiny fingers on the coveted toy, he burrowed under the blanket and went to sleep.

Once again, I'd proven myself a hopeless parent.

I tried to put my woes out of my mind as Giuseppe's delivered a piping hot pepperoni with extra peppers. Emmy introduced me to the pleasure of their extra deep crusts when she came for my audition, and I hadn't been able to resist their lure. After spending half my life cooking for others, having someone else bring my food was a guilty pleasure, one I'd indulged in every week since I arrived in Boston, although I usually waited until I was alone at the weekends.

We spread out the pizza plus a side order of chicken wings on the breakfast bar in the kitchen and hopped up on the high stools. In between mouthfuls topped with gooey cheese, I told Sofia about my day.

"Wow, Jansen sounds like an asshole."

"He's just dedicated. It's only a problem because he wants to inflict his practice regime on everyone else." When I stepped back and looked at the situation rationally, I couldn't be too harsh on him. In Japan, his work ethic would have been applauded, but I wanted my life to be about more than the daily grind.

"Even so...he shouldn't be pushing you and Jude around like that, even if Jude does need to put a bit more effort in."

"It'll be easier once my own piano arrives. I'll be able to escape home and avoid him."

"At least you've got this Lincoln guy looking out for you in the meantime."

I'd described the way he stepped in when Jansen got difficult, but not how he held my hand afterwards. I hadn't got my feelings about that straight in my own mind, and this whole confiding-in-others thing was new to me. One step at a time.

"I know. Let's hope Jansen got the message. I don't think I could stand the stress of him every day I need to practice at Holborn."

In my room that evening, I caught a glimpse of my silhouette in the mirror fixed to the wall next to the wardrobe. With all the hurry to move in, I hadn't got around to taking it down yet, and in daylight I'd trained myself to close my eyes as I walked past. It was bad enough having to look at the scars on my wrists every day, without seeing the crisscross of cuts that marred my body as well. Each one brought back a memory, every thin line a reminder of a night worse than the last.

While most of the guards gave up on me by the time I turned twenty, one persisted for two more years. Every time he raped me, he carved into my body, his hand clamped over my mouth to stop me from waking everyone with my screams.

"I am the artist," he'd whisper as the blade flicked over my skin. "And you are my masterpiece."

I was an abomination.

Over the years I'd become adept at doing things in the dark—showering, getting dressed, even sex. Hisashi's father never saw me naked, not once. He knew why and never pushed it. We both bore the scars from that place.

Tonight I slipped on a long nightgown and burrowed under the quilt, craving sleep. Every time I closed my eyes I played a game of Russian roulette, dreams versus nightmares, and I'd risk the bullet because dreams were the only place I saw the man I loved now. Would tonight be a good night or a bad one? Would I wake up screaming? Or see his handsome face once more?

I laid my head back on the fluffy pillow, concentrating on my breathing, a meditation I performed every night. Usually it sent me off, but tonight my mind stayed busy with a replay of earlier events. Jude's refusal to practice. Jansen forcing me back to the piano. Lincoln standing up for me, holding my hand, making me feel safe. How could I thank him properly for what he'd done? Sitting in his room earlier, I'd gone all tongue-tied, and my paltry efforts at showing my appreciation were inadequate.

After twenty minutes of fidgeting I gave in and snatched my phone off the nightstand. The picture of Hisashi on the screen cast a soft peach glow over the room before I called up the contacts menu and scrolled through it. Linc. Those four letters set my heart pounding, and I felt his hand on mine again. The house was cool, but I pushed the quilt down as a hot flash ran through me, setting my nerve endings on fire. How could a name on a screen have such an effect on me?

My fingers trembled as I tried to come up with a

suitable message.

Akari: Dear Lincoln, I wish to thank you...

Scrap that. Far too formal.

Akari: Hi Linc, thanks for helping me out tonight. I wasn't sure I'd ever get away otherwise!

Nope. Too bland. I might as well have been thanking a store assistant for handing me my bags.

Akari: Linc, I didn't thank you properly earlier for helping me, because I wasn't sure what to say. You've probably noticed I'm not so good at dealing with strangers. If you hadn't stepped in I'd still be there now, asleep over the keys while Jansen played on without me. I truly am grateful for what you did, and I hope it didn't ruin your evening too much. Akari.

I read it back quickly, muttering to myself, and it still sounded superficial but I didn't know what else to write. Before I chickened out altogether, I pressed send.

Tossing the phone onto the spare pillow next to me, I snuggled back under the covers, the warmth from earlier replaced by a sudden chill. Was it appropriate to text a man so late at night? It wasn't like I'd ever had experience with this. I went back to my measured breathing, but it didn't help, and when the phone buzzed I snatched it up.

Linc: My evening could never be ruined by spending time with you. Sleep tight. L.

I read his words ten times over, searching for a meaning that probably wasn't there. Eventually, I did as instructed and drifted off, still clutching the phone in my hand, as though it would bring me closer to the man who wrote the words still blinking on the screen.

Hisashi's father didn't come to me that night, but somebody else visited my dreams instead.

I shook my head as hot water pounded me in the morning, trying to clear my mind of a Hisashi-induced headache and thoughts I shouldn't be having about a man I barely knew.

My peaceful thoughts of Lincoln had been interrupted at three a.m. by Hisashi's cries on the baby monitor. I'd scrambled out of bed and changed his diaper, but he didn't quiet down until four, and after that I couldn't get back to sleep again.

Things didn't get any easier after I pulled on a pair of jeans and a sweater then flicked on the light, only to see the message icon on my phone blinking. A message from Lincoln? Or Linc as he'd called himself? What did he want?

Fingers shaking, I opened it and found a picture of a puppy with *Smile - let them know that today you're stronger than you were yesterday* written next to it.

I couldn't help it—the corners of my mouth curved up into a grin as I slipped my feet into a pair of ballet pumps, not just because what Linc said was right, but because he'd woken up and sent me such a sweet message.

His words kept me going through my classes in the morning, all the way through to the evening when I trudged to the practice room again. Jansen and Jude we're already there when I arrived, Jude looking about as thrilled as I felt.

My heart sank as I took my seat at the piano, but when I lifted the lid above the keys I found a post-it note stuck to the inside.

Don't forget to smile! :)

I did, earning a curious glance from Jude before I turned away to get the sheet music from my bag. I didn't need it—I already knew the piece by heart—but having it there gave me an excuse not to look at people. Yes, I was that much of a coward.

With Lincoln's note above the keys for me to see every time I glanced down, three hours of Jansen's barbs went faster than I'd dared to hope. The only disappointment was that when I left, there was no sign of Linc himself. I'd wanted to thank him for his messages, and, well, I'd just hoped to see him.

All the way home, I tried to think of the right words to send him, but by the time the car pulled up outside my home, I still hadn't managed it. Then the phone vibrated in my hand.

Linc: Got held up tonight - all the excitement of a blocked toilet. Hope things went alright with Il Duce and the slacker and you managed to keep smiling. L.

He'd done it again. I giggled, even if Mussolini had been Italian and Jansen was Dutch. On impulse, I paused in the hallway and snapped a picture of myself smiling and sent it before I convinced myself it was a bad idea.

By the time I reached Hisashi's bedroom to kiss him goodnight, I'd got a photo back of Linc displaying a row of perfect white teeth, together with a message: *You've made me smile too. Sleep well.*

That night, I did.

CHAPTER 14

ON THURSDAY EVENING, I went to practice prepared. As I already knew every note of the piece, I left the crutch of my sheet music in my bag and placed it near the door, next to Jude's backpack. Was he planning to make a run for it as well?

It appeared the answer was yes. After an hour of Jansen's mutterings, he stood up. "Gotta run, man."

"You can't. It's the recital tomorrow, and you haven't played the last twelve bars properly once yet."

"I'll get up early and play it through in the morning. People are waiting for me in town." He turned and gave me a wink. "Karaoke night at Club Lagonda, if you fancy coming."

I hurriedly shook my head, unable to think of anything worse than getting drunk and attempting to sing in front of hundreds of strangers. But I used the interruption to edge towards the door myself.

"I need to go too." Before Jansen could reply I added, "I've played the last bit perfectly so no need to worry."

With two of us dissenting, I saw Jansen didn't know which way to turn. I took advantage of his confusion to make a break for it, grabbing my bag as I got near the door and jogging down the hallway.

Footsteps sounded behind me, but I didn't stop to

see whose they were. Fearing Jansen had decided to follow, I passed the elevator and ran into the stairwell. At the first floor I hesitated. As I hadn't been sure I'd escape, my driver wasn't waiting, so I needed a place to hide until he got there. The sound of the door above opening spurred my feet into action, and I ran down the next flight of stairs to the basement.

The place was bigger than I remembered, and without Linc to guide me, my chest tightened as my breathing threatened to get out of control.

"Just breathe," I whispered, placing my hand on my chest to calm myself. My footsteps clicked on the tile floor as I hurried along the corridor, trying to recall which of the closed doors led to Linc's palace, as he called it.

Finally, I recognised the torn poster of last year's graduation concert and pushed inside, seeing Linc's bag next to the chair. I sank down onto the seat, letting out a breath I didn't realise I'd been holding.

"Didn't need my help tonight, then?"

I jumped so violently the chair shot out from under me, and the only thing that kept me from hitting the floor was Linc's arm under my back. I grabbed his other hand with both of mine to steady myself.

"Sorry, didn't mean to startle you," he said, retrieving the seat and lowering me back into it. "I called out to you in the stairwell. Didn't you hear me?"

I shook my head. At that point I'd only been thinking of getting away.

"Hardly surprising with the amount of noise you were making." He broke into a grin as he crouched beside me. "You wouldn't make a very good ninja."

The idea of me creeping around in black, Emmystyle, was enough to make me burst into laughter. In fact, it wasn't until I looked down that I realised my hands were still gripping his, and that his was resting on my thigh. Even a week ago I'd have panicked, but today I willed myself to stay steady, and apart from a wobbly intake of breath I managed it.

"I thought Jansen was behind me."

"Nope, just me. I came to check on you, and you shot past like the fires of hell were burning under your ass. Il Duce was too busy arguing with the slacker to come after you, but I figured that dude could look after himself."

My shoulders slumped forwards with relief. "Thank goodness."

"So why did you come down here? I thought you weren't keen on basements."

This was one of those times when my inability to lie had me at a disadvantage. My voice dropped to a whisper as I told him the truth. "I thought you might be here, and you make me feel safe."

He stiffened, and for a second I thought I'd scared him off. Men don't like emotional women, right? But then he covered my two hands with his free one and gently squeezed. "I'm glad to hear it. You come here any time you need to, okay?"

I nodded, unable to speak at his kindness. My heart was beating so loudly I felt sure he must be able to hear it.

"Do you need to call your driver?"

Again, I nodded. "Yes, please."

He let go of me, leaving my hands cold in my lap, and pushed the clunky old phone towards me. "Here you go."

The driver said he'd be with me in five minutes, and I almost told him to go around the block a few times. But it wouldn't be fair of me to take up Linc's evening— he needed to get home as well. Did he have a family waiting for him? A wife? A girlfriend? My eyes darted towards his hand, checking for a ring. Nothing, thank goodness, but surely he must have a girlfriend? Someone as damn sweet as him couldn't be alone.

"He won't be long."

I replaced the receiver, anxiety building in my gut as a strange army of feelings marched through. Sickness, then fear, then the flutters I used to get whenever I saw Hisashi's father. Oh hell, this wasn't good. Panic slammed into me as I realised what they meant. I liked Linc. Really liked him. And that thought had me pushing the chair back as I tried to get the space to breathe. I needed oxygen, but my lungs weren't cooperating.

"What's wrong?" Linc reached for my hand again, and I let him take it, limp in his grasp.

"Nothing."

"You're shaking. Did I do something to upset you?"

"No. I, um, I think I'm just nervous about the recital tomorrow. I mean, what if Jansen's right and we didn't practice enough?"

"You've done plenty. Go home, make sure you get some sleep and eat a good breakfast. You'll knock their socks off when you play."

Sleep. It was all very well Linc telling me to sleep but how could I when his face haunted my dreams? Not

Hisashi's father but this newcomer, and the guilt that I was tarnishing the memory of the man who saved my life and showed me love kept me awake half the night. By the time the sun rose I was a wreck.

"Nervous?" Sofia asked, over breakfast.

I grabbed onto the excuse. "Very much. I've never played in front of such a large audience before."

"With the amount of practice you've done, you'll get top marks."

"I hope so." Or Jansen would fire a rocket up my ass.

In morning classes, I blocked everything from my mind but the teachers speaking at the front, concentrating on taking notes in my literature seminar then on putting together harmonies in the theory class that followed. That strategy worked until lunchtime, when my phone buzzed with a text, and I knew it was from Linc before I even looked at the screen. Emmy and her husband already sent a good luck video, my parents and brother called me last night, and Bradley sent enough flowers to start my own store. There was nobody else it could be.

Linc: Smile and be strong. As soon as people hear you play, they'll all smile too.

I didn't share his confidence, but as I made my way to the stage in the auditorium, carrying my sheet music in front of me like a shield, I forced the corners of my mouth upwards. I couldn't fool myself, but I could try to persuade the others I was happy. Linc said I wasn't a ninja, but the butterflies in my stomach had armed themselves with throwing stars and they liked to practice as much as Jansen did.

It wasn't until I raised my hands and started to play

that I began to breathe again, and when I flipped over to the second page where I'd stuck Linc's note reminding me to smile, I relaxed for the first time that day. I'd go so far as to say I was enjoying myself, until I caught movement out of the corner of my eye.

A man slipped into the back of the room, wearing jeans and a long-sleeved shirt, and without his grey overalls it took me a few seconds to realise it was Linc. He'd come to watch me!

"Akari! What are you doing?" Jansen's furious hiss brought me to my senses, and I realised the others had played on without me.

By the time I worked out where they'd got to, I'd missed nearly a whole line of music and mutterings in the audience told me that hadn't gone unnoticed. Cheeks heating, I fought back tears as we finished the piece then took my place in the second row beside Jude. I let him sit between me and Jansen although that only prolonged the inevitable.

"What the fuck was wrong with you?" Jansen asked, as soon as the last group played and the dean finished his speech.

"I just lost my place. I'm sorry."

"It was him, wasn't it? The janitor? I saw him walk in right when you screwed up. What the hell are you doing with him?"

"Nothing, I swear." But I knew my blush said otherwise.

"You're stupid. You've got real talent and you're wasting it gallivanting with the hired help. You need to get your act together before you screw up all our grades."

"I will, I promise. I'll practice more next time," I

replied, but I was left speaking to his back as he stormed out.

Jude stood beside me, watching him leave. "Ignore him. Everybody's allowed to make mistakes."

"I shouldn't have got distracted."

"Hey, if a hot babe walked in, I'd have stopped playing as well." He picked up his cello and grinned. "It's over now, so at least we can enjoy our weekend without little Hitler breathing down our necks."

I followed him out, head bowed. Despite his lack of practice and love of the Boston nightlife, he'd played the piece perfectly. He passed every test in the other classes we shared too. Yes, Jude performed when it mattered, whereas I screwed up with astonishing regularity.

I'd got halfway along the hallway, still berating myself, when I felt a presence beside me.

"I'm sorry," Linc said. "I didn't mean to put you off."

"It was all my fault. I've been struggling to concentrate."

His raised eyebrow told me he didn't quite believe what I said, but he nodded, accepting it. "Anything I can do to help?"

A vision of him standing shirtless in front of me popped into my mind and my eyes widened. Oh no, I was not allowing myself to go there. "Apart from turning back the clock so I can start again, no."

"I'm all out of time machines, but how about a coffee?" He glanced at his watch. "If you don't have anywhere to be, that is."

"I'm done for the day." I studied my shoes, unable to meet his eyes. "Yes, I'd like a coffee."

I thought he meant in his palace, but it turned out he'd finished work as well. "Management swaps our shifts around each week. They like to keep us on our toes," he said, as he led me out of the building to a café a couple of blocks away.

That explained his attire. In well-worn denim and a soft flannel shirt, he looked quite different to the man I'd grown used to seeing at Holborn. Only the scruffy beard gave him away, and I couldn't help wondering what he'd look like without it.

He held the door open for me, and I ducked under his arm and went inside, spotting a table on the far side where a couple had just got up to leave. Linc saw it too and nodded towards it.

"You grab the table, I'll get drinks. What do you want?"

"Cappuccino with caramel syrup, please."

He nodded then headed for the counter, muttering something about "too sweet." Well, I couldn't help my sugar addiction. Sometimes it was the only thing that got me through the day. When he came back, he must have relented, because the tray also held two plates, one with a chocolate brownie and the other with a banana muffin. I prayed the healthier option was for him, and I needn't have worried because he slid the gooey delight in my direction.

"Thought you might be hungry as well."

"Thanks. I didn't eat lunch." The ninja butterflies hadn't allowed me to, but now the horror was over I broke a piece off the brownie and shoved it in my mouth.

An awkward silence followed, as Linc took a mouthful of coffee then leaned on his hands, watching me.

Finally, he spoke. "I wanted to check you were okay, you know, because with the weekend I won't see you for a couple of days now. I've noticed you fret about things."

"I'll be okay."

"You have somebody you can talk to at home?"

"I live with, uh, a...my son's nanny."

He did a double take and put down his cup. "Your son?"

"Hisashi. He's sixteen months old."

"And what about...? Forget it, it's none of my business."

"His father?"

Linc nodded.

"His father isn't around."

If I'd thought the first silence was awkward, the second seemed to last forever. I turned to the brownie for moral support. Chocolate didn't judge. Chocolate understood.

When I could stand it no longer, I asked the question that had plagued me for days. "How about you? Do you have someone to talk to?"

"Like a priest?"

"Not exactly."

"An old high school buddy?"

"That wasn't what I was thinking of."

He cocked his head on one side. "I don't understand."

"I meant a girlfriend," I blurted. "Do you have a girlfriend?" Too late I caught the twinkle in his eye. "You were messing with me." I didn't know whether to sink into the floor or run out the door.

He chuckled then melted my insides with his smile. "I'm single. The army isn't kind to relationships, and since I got out I haven't found anyone who'll put up with me."

"You were in the army?"

"Yeah, for ten years."

"Why?"

"What do you mean?"

"Why were you in the army?" I'd seen too many men seduced by guns. They thought there was glory in carrying a weapon, and by the time they realised the death and destruction they caused it was too late. They'd crossed to the dark side or lost their lives to some misguided cause.

Only when I asked that question Linc's eyes took on a depth I'd never seen before. Pain leached out of them, and this time it was me who reached out to take his hand. "What is it?" I whispered. "What's wrong?"

His voice dropped as he spoke, not looking at me but at some random spot over my shoulder. "When I was eight years old, my daddy killed my momma while me and my two brothers slept in the next room. I swore when I grew up I'd do what I could to keep people safe, and I did that by serving my country."

Ohhhh hell. Why did I have to be so nosey? I stroked his fingers, which had gone cold under my touch. "I'm so sorry. I didn't mean to pry."

He let out a long sigh, then with seemingly some effort, focused back on my face. "It was a long time ago now. I've learned to live with it."

"What about your brothers?" Why couldn't I shut up?

"Joel never got over it. He died of an overdose at

eighteen while I was serving overseas." Linc inhaled deeply and closed his eyes, and I wished I could do something to ease his pain. "He hid his addiction until the day I got the call telling me he was in a coma, but the stupid bastard never did wake up. Drew's a doctor in Vancouver. Paediatrics."

"I'm sorry." A tear leaked down my cheek, and Linc reached out and brushed it away. "Don't cry. My past isn't a part of your future."

Wasn't it? Because that past made him who he was, and whatever future I had, I saw Linc in it. "I wish those things hadn't happened to your family."

"Me too, sweetheart. Me too." He stroked my cheek then pushed his chair back. "I've lost my appetite, I'm afraid. You want me to walk you back to school?"

"I can call my driver to pick me up here." I fumbled for my phone, not wanting to risk going back to Holborn in case Jansen was still lurking somewhere.

"I'd offer you a lift but I've only got a bike."

"You cycle everywhere?"

"Motorbike. Not much to hold onto on the back except me, and if you don't like being touched it's not a great way to travel."

"I can get my driver to drop you back to your bike?"

"Thanks, but I need the walk. It'll help clear my head."

I wished that worked for me. I could go twice round the equator on foot and my mind would never be empty. Instead, I watched from the car as Linc set off, hoping he'd find the peace he sought.

CHAPTER 15

MONDAY MORNING BROUGHT new assignments. This time I'd be playing Brahms' Piano Trio No. 3 in C Minor with my two favourite classmates. Jansen had thoughtfully created a timetable for us, which included a minimum of two hours of practice each day. It didn't look like there was much room for manoeuvre in his schedule—he'd printed it out onto cards and laminated them.

"This is worse than last time," I whispered to Jude.

"I know. Reckon I'm going to get a doctor's note or something. The dude's crazy."

At this rate the next time I saw Hisashi I'd be sending him off to kindergarten and he'd be calling Sofia mama. I needed to think of something. Maybe Linc could help? Although I was a bit nervous of speaking to him. On Saturday I'd sent him a message apologising for causing the upset the previous day, but apart from a generic "It's okay" reply, I hadn't heard from him all weekend. What if our fledgling friendship was irreparably damaged?

By the end of the morning's lessons I couldn't stand the worry any longer. I planned to skip lunch and look for him. I needed to know how he was feeling about things.

Except the faculty had other ideas.

"Akari, the dean has requested you go and see him in his office now," Dr. Vasilyevich said, as I was walking towards the door.

"What about?"

His glare told me such trivialities weren't his concern. "I do not know, but I wouldn't advise being late."

Was it about my error in the recital on Friday? Because one of my classmates managed to play the same page twice, and she didn't get called in. In fact, that was her laughing with her group on the way to the cafeteria.

Cursing under my breath that I wouldn't be able to speak to Linc, I made my way to the dean's office, more peeved than nervous for once, although the ten minutes his secretary made me wait on a hard plastic seat outside didn't help matters. Eventually, the door swung open and she waved me inside.

"Take a seat, Miss Takeda," the dean said.

I did so, trying to get comfortable on a chair made for aesthetics rather than sitting on, and failing. "Is this about the recital?"

"No, this is about what happened after the recital."

"Huh?"

"I'm sure you're familiar with clause 137.6 on page ninety-three of the student handbook."

Oh, intimately. I studied it every night between Jansen's insane practice regime and caring for my son. "Uh, what does it say?"

"It expressly forbids any sort of relationship between staff at Holborn and the students. That isn't limited to faculty, but includes support staff as well."

"I don't understand."

"I have it on good authority that you went out for dinner with a member of the janitorial staff on Friday evening." He glanced down at the notepad in front of him. "A Lincoln Macbride."

Oh shit. "No, we didn't go for dinner."

"Three people report you left the premises together, as well as another who saw you in a restaurant. I also checked the CCTV cameras at the front of the school for confirmation."

Now what should I say? Working on the assumption Linc would have been called into a similar meeting, not to mention my terrible lying ability, I'd have to stick with the truth and be as vague as possible.

"I was a little upset over the mistake I made in the recital, and he suggested getting something to eat or drink might help me to feel better. Also I hadn't eaten lunch, so I was hungry."

"Where did you go for this meal?"

"It wasn't a meal, just coffee and cake. Some café a few blocks away, but I don't remember the name. Linc... Lincoln, he chose it."

"And this was the first time you left the school grounds with him?"

"Yes."

"What time did you finish this...snack?"

"Uh, maybe six thirty? I didn't look at my watch."

"And did you return to the school?"

"No, my driver picked me up from the cafe, but I think Lincoln came back."

The dean leaned back in his chair, hands steepled in front of him. "Miss Takeda, here at Holborn we take the non-fraternisation rule very seriously. Any slip-ups could lead to favouritism over grades, non-regulation booking of practice rooms or students being in the building during hours of closure. I suggest you read the relevant sections in the school handbook very carefully because if I hear of this happening again it will be a disciplinary offence, for you and Mr. Macbride. Do you understand?"

"Yes."

He gave me a tight smile. "Then you may go. I hope not to see you in here like this again."

"You won't." Because if Linc wanted to meet for coffee again, we'd just have to be careful we weren't spotted. While a more sensible girl may have heeded the dean's warning, I'd spent fifteen years being ordered around by a man whose idea of a disciplinary offence involved losing limbs. Beside him, the head of Holborn was a kitten. Claws? What claws? I was damn well sick of being told what to do.

The instant I got out, I headed for the nearest bathroom and locked myself into a stall. At least I had privacy in there. Fingers moving as fast as they could, I typed out a message to Linc.

Akari: The dean just told me off for going for coffee on Friday. Has he said anything to you?

The reply was almost instantaneous.

Linc: I saw you go in after me. What did you say?

Akari: Just that I was upset after the recital and we went for coffee together.

Linc: More or less what I said. I got a verbal warning but nothing more unless it happens again.

Akari: I'm so sorry.

Linc: Don't be. I knew there was a risk but I couldn't keep away from you. I'm just sorry you got called in as well.

He couldn't keep away? Palms sweating, I tried to think of a reply, one that conveyed my own feelings but without coming across as ridiculously needy. I'd never been a risk taker, but Emmy told me the real risk was to do nothing because that way you'd never truly live. And given that I'd felt more alive in the last two weeks than the year that came before them I knew I had to take a chance.

Akari: Even if I had read the stupid handbook I'd have gone anyway. Next time we'll need to leave separately and check nobody follows.

Nothing. Silence. Two minutes ticked by and Linc didn't reply. Panicking, I sent another message.

Akari: If you want there to be a next time?

I sat on the closed toilet lid staring at the phone, willing it to light up.

Linc: Too damn right I want a next time. Give me a minute. Thinking about logistics.

Not long after, a map arrived, showing the way to a bar six blocks away. Not the kind of place I'd normally go, but if Linc was there I'd have to give it a try.

Linc: You've got practice until eight, right?

Akari: How do you know?

Linc: Il Duce booked the room every evening for the rest of the semester.

Oh hell.

Akari: Yes, I have practice until eight. Unless Jansen decides to carry on through the night which is entirely possible.

Linc: You'll finish at eight, trust me. Can you walk to the bar? I swear I'll be right behind you, even if you don't see me.

I'd promised Emmy I wouldn't go out alone without

bodyguards, but no way was I going to call her up and explain the situation. She'd probably scare Linc off by having a team of investigators rake through his life then send out a plague of her men to follow me everywhere.

Akari: I can do that.

Linc: Then I'll see you later.

"Boyfriend not here tonight?" The look of triumph on Jansen's face when he caught me looking at my watch left me under no illusion as to who'd reported Linc and me to the dean.

"He's not my boyfriend, as you well know."

Quarter to eight, and Jansen showed no sign of letting up. I'd been waiting for Jude to make a move, hoping to follow him out, but so far he seemed unusually subdued.

"That's what you say. Shall we go again from the top?"

I started to play, my mind on other things. Trust him, Linc said, and I tried to, but where was he?

I found out at five to eight.

"Holy hell," Jude said. "That sounds like a power saw."

Sure enough, when Jude yanked the door open, there was Linc, bent over a portable workbench. He grinned up at us. "Don't mind me, people. It's time these skirting boards got replaced. Figure if I spend a bit of time each night for the next month, it'll be done."

Jansen's face went red while Jude muttered a silent thank you to the heavens.

"You can't do this," Jansen sputtered. "I'll report it to the dean."

Linc produced a sheet of paper from his pocket. "The dean signed off on the work order. I happened to be in to see him this afternoon, and we had a nice chat about it. He thought renewing some of the woodwork was an excellent idea."

"You...You..."

"Yes?"

Jansen backed into the room, forcing Jude and I back inside. "That man is unreasonable." He pointed at me. "Do something."

I held my hands up. "I can't. Clause 137.6 of the student handbook forbids me from speaking to him."

The sound of the door slamming behind Jansen was sweet music to my ears, and I turned to Jude in relief. "Thank goodness. No more ridiculous finishes for a while."

He gathered up his cello. "Thank your boyfriend for me, would you?"

"He's not my boyfriend."

"Sure he isn't."

Twenty-nine years old, and the last time I'd walked down a street alone was sixteen years ago and look where that landed me. But Linc asked me to trust him, and he'd already come through for me once tonight. I had to believe he was watching over me.

The moon threw long, jagged shadows across the sidewalk as I scurried along, listening for footfalls behind. I heard nothing, which only made me walk faster. By the time I saw the lit sign of the Blue Moon bar up ahead, I was practically running.

I paused for a few seconds to get my breathing under control before I pushed inside. Even before I opened the door, the vibrations of the music inside ran through me. Someone in there had no concept of volume.

No sooner had I stepped over the threshold, I felt rather than saw Linc at my back. He didn't touch me, but he got so close I could feel his body heat, then the soft whisper of breath as he bent to speak in my ear. "Sorry, I didn't realise they'd have live music on. It's never usually this busy. You want to go somewhere else?"

Yes, but at the same time I desperately wanted to behave like a normal person. Everyone else around me was laughing or smiling or dancing, and I refused to let fear beat me down yet again. I quickly shook my head before I could change my mind.

"In that case, head for the bar. We'll get a couple of drinks."

Nerves buzzing from his proximity, I walked hesitantly towards the mass of bodies in front of me, wondering how I was going to get through them. Then Linc's arms came around me like a protective cage as he gently pushed me forwards. Before I had time to panic we'd made it to the wooden counter, and Linc placed one hand on the edge either side of me, preventing the jostling crowd from coming any closer.

"What do you want?" Closer to the music, he almost had to shout to make himself heard.

How about a medal and a round of applause? "A glass of white wine." I deserved at least that.

"Not sure they serve wine in here. Beer, spirits or soft drink?"

I'd never tried beer, but this was a day for doing new things, and it seemed appropriate for this sort of establishment. "Beer."

He raised an eyebrow. "Okay."

He ordered a cola for himself then looked around for a table. The band was on a break, and people milled around everywhere. After a few minutes of waiting, we ended up in the back corner with me perched on the only free stool.

"Are you sure you don't want to sit down?" I asked.

"I'm good. No, here with you, I'm more than good."

"Thanks for getting me out of practice. You should have seen Jansen's face when you started up the saw."

"Wish I'd been there. The downside is that I really do have to replace the skirting boards, but I figured it was worth a few late nights."

"Is there anything I can do to make it up to you?"

"Smile." He reached out and traced the contours of my lips with his index finger. "Just smile."

When his hand dropped, I caught it in mine and held it in my lap, afraid that if I let it go the moment would end. The band struck up again, making conversation impossible, but we didn't need to speak. Just being near Linc was enough to turn the day from a journey through hell to a dream of paradise.

CHAPTER 16

TONIGHT LINC PLANNED to get work done on the skirting boards—he messaged me earlier to let me know. Jansen, being bloody minded, insisted on us practising through the screams of the power saw even when we could hardly hear ourselves play.

Eventually Jude refused to go on, citing a migraine, and Jansen didn't try to argue with him.

"Same time tomorrow," he said. "We don't want more mistakes in the next recital, do we?" He stared at me as he said that.

"I'll be here," I said through gritted teeth.

Linc had bits of wood stacked against the wall when I left, and I snuck him a smile. If only we didn't have to go through this stupid charade, I could go and talk to him, but while I'd risk my own position, I didn't want to jeopardise his job. He caught my eye, checked behind me for watching spies, then waggled his eyebrows and blew me a kiss before looking back at his tools as Jansen stepped out of the room.

My stomach flipped, and I had to refrain from fanning myself. How could Linc do that and act so nonchalant about it? Beyond frustrated, I stomped off, already composing a message to send to him in my head. No, not a message, a picture. Alone in the elevator, I blew my own kiss into the camera lens then sent it to him. Take that!

With the pressing business of winding Linc up out of the way, I called my driver once I got to the atrium.

"I'm afraid I'll be delayed, ma'am," he replied, and I heard the honk of a car horn in the background.

"What's happened? Are you okay?"

"Fine, ma'am, but I'm on the freeway, and there's been an accident up ahead. Traffic's at a standstill. If you prefer, I can call the control room and get them to send someone else."

"No, it's fine. I'll wait." I was enough of a burden on Blackwood without taking another of their staff for the evening.

I settled onto one of the uncomfortable ornamental benches and stared at the phone screen. Should I have sent that photo? Was it too much?

"Still here?" Linc's voice came from behind me, but when I turned he maintained a good distance. His eyes flicked to the right, and I knew why—the red eye of the watching camera blinked down at us, recording evidence of our interaction.

"My driver's stuck in traffic."

"On the freeway? I heard about a big accident on the radio. A lorry jack-knifed and eight cars went into the side of it."

"Shit, those poor people. Looks like I'm stuck here. And the irony is Jansen's gone home."

"How about calling a cab?"

"I don't like being around strangers." Plus, Emmy would go nuts if she found out. "I'd rather wait."

"You want me to come in the cab with you?"

"You'd do that?"

"Of course, but it'd have to pick me up down the

block so nobody sees. Hang on, I'll call the company I use on occasion."

A minute later, he hung up. "Well, it seems like everyone else has had the same idea. They can't send anyone for at least half an hour, and apparently there's been a fire downtown and the city's in gridlock."

"I'd better call my nanny and let her know I'll be late. My son will already be in bed, but I don't want her to worry."

"Unless you're feeling brave?"

"Huh?"

"I've got the bike outside."

Did I dare? I should have been horrified at the thought, but instead heat pooled in my stomach as I imagined pressing up against Linc, his butt between my thighs. He'd said before that I'd need to hold on to him, and I pictured my arms wrapped around his waist as he gunned the engine. A tremble ran through me, and it took a few seconds for me to recognise it not as fear, but lust.

Only one man had made me shiver like that before, and a wave of guilt washed over me, extinguishing the heat. Even though he'd died, I still felt loyalty towards him, and what would people say if they knew I had feelings for another man?

I frowned, trying to sort out my thoughts. Hisashi's father was a memory now, whereas Linc was very real and standing in front of me, waiting for an answer.

His eyes got me. Even from ten metres away, they sucked me into their depths. "Could you give me a lift?"

"You sure?" he asked softly.

"I'm scared," I whispered. "But I still need to do this."

"I'll go and get my extra helmet. Meet me on the sidewalk to the right of the main entrance in ten minutes. The cameras only cover the left side."

"Okay."

"And Akari?"

"Yes?"

"You can give me the real version of that picture you sent before you go home tonight."

Ten minutes, and I spent it pacing the tiles like a madwoman. Had I gone crazy? I'd agreed to sit on the back of a death trap, and all because my fingers wanted to feel Linc's muscles. I'd gone undeniably mad. Completely psycho. But did he have a six-pack?

When the time was up, I fidgeted in the darkness at the appointed spot until I heard the roar of a powerful engine coming from the parking lot, and a few seconds later Linc drew up alongside me and put his feet down. The sporty bike was bright red, with *Ducati* stencilled along the side.

"You ready?"

I nodded, not trusting myself to speak. He passed me a helmet, which came up a little big, but he helped me fasten the strap under my chin and pronounced it would do.

"I'm not planning on going fast, not with you on the back. Where do you live?"

I told him, then asked, "How do I get on?"

"Just swing your leg over the back. I'll hold the bike steady."

A simple hop, and Linc's luscious cheeks nestled between my thighs. I reached gingerly around his waist and clasped my hands in front of his stomach, waiting. Oh yeah, he did have that six-pack I'd been wondering about. Maybe even an eight-pack.

"Okay?"

"I think so."

He took that to mean yes and started the engine. Vibrations. I hadn't even thought of the vibrations. They shot through my core where I perched on the leather seat, acting as a touch-paper to my libido. Before I could calm myself down, Linc shot off and my arms tightened around him involuntarily.

Wind whipped through my hair as we flew through the streets, and I may have shrieked a little. When we pulled up at the first stoplight, Linc put one hand over mine, clasping me against his stomach.

"Having fun?"

"I'm not sure if fun's the right word for it."

"You want to stop?"

"No."

More than anything I'd missed this closeness, this contact with another human being. Even though there were several layers of clothing between us, I felt a connection I couldn't explain. Arms rigid, I clung onto Linc for the rest of the ride until all too soon, we arrived at my home. Between the throb of the engine and the ripple of Linc's muscles, I was consumed with unfulfilled need, like being stuck on a precipice I wanted to jump off, but with feet that refused to move.

"We're here," he announced.

"I think my legs have stopped working."

He laughed as he put the bike on its stand then hopped off and lifted me to the ground. If it wasn't for his arm around my waist, holding me steady, I'd have buckled to the concrete.

"I'm proud of you. You only screamed four times."

Yes, once at the start, twice when Linc overtook other vehicles and once when I had a mini-orgasm in the fast lane. I'd never admit to that last one, though.

"I had fun."

He pulled his helmet off then helped me out of mine. "Good. I want you to hear those words from you more often."

"You will."

Linc swung his leg back over the saddle, and I held my breath as he reached out to tuck a lock of hair behind my ear. "Goodnight, sweetheart."

"Goodnight, Linc." I turned to go inside, distinctly lacking in enthusiasm.

"Hey!"

"What?"

"Are you forgetting the photo?"

I bent forward, puckered up and blew him a kiss. "See you tomorrow." Hell, I'd turned into a wanton woman, and what's more, I enjoyed it. Seeing his smile and feeling happier, I jogged into the apartment building, wondering what my dreams would bring tonight.

CHAPTER 17

"I HEAR YOU went out with the janitor again," Jude said as we walked into our yoga class on Thursday. I'd changed in a toilet stall with my eyes closed, well away from the curious eyes of my classmates.

"What? Who told you that? Jansen?"

"Nope, some girl in my cello class. If it helps, she reckons he's got a nice butt."

I knew that already. "What exactly did she say?"

"Just that someone saw you going into that new pizza place on the next block last night. Is it nice?"

"How would I know? I didn't go."

"Oh. Where did he take you then?"

"Nowhere! I went straight home after practice, and I was so tired I fell asleep halfway through a repeat of *CSI*."

Jude gave a hearty laugh. "Looks like the rumour mill's working overtime again. At least it takes some of the heat off me."

Jude wandered off to a spot at the back, and my fingers pecked furiously at the screen on my phone as I sent a message to Linc to let him know what happened. When class started a few minutes later, the tension in my muscles made me twist my shoulder as I fell out of a half-moon pose and landed in a heap on the mat. There were sniggers from the back as I picked myself up, and I cursed the person who thought it was a good idea to tie yourself up in knots in the name of wellbeing. The one position I could do properly was corpse pose, and that was only because I was too exhausted to move.

And I still had to deal with the added stress of Jansen's despotic tendencies.

I checked my phone on the way out of the sports hall, and sure enough, Linc had replied.

Linc: Really? I heard we went out to the posh French place. Pizza makes it sound like I cheaped out.

Akari: And you'd never do that?

Linc: I wouldn't care if I ate a sandwich on a park bench as long as it was with you.

Akari: So you're saying you want to take me out to sit on a bench?

Linc: No, I want to take you somewhere obscenely expensive and feed you lobster and chocolate mousse. I want to hear you moan like you did eating that brownie the other day.

Akari: I did not moan.

Linc: Yes, you did, sweetheart.

Okay, maybe I had just a little.

Akari: So tell me more about this imaginary date. What are you going to wear?

Linc: At the beginning or the end?

I stopped dead in the middle of the corridor, rigid, and somebody walked into my back. I turned to see a girl I recognised from aural training picking up a pile of papers.

"I'm so sorry, that was my fault. Let me help." I bent and grabbed a music score.

"No worries, we all zone out sometimes. Hey, it's

you. Is it true you're dating the janitor?"

I straightened up, my shoulder protesting. "No, it's not. Someone's spreading lies about me." Only with his messages burning up the screen in my hand, it felt like me who was lying.

"Too bad, he's kinda cute." She stuffed everything back in her bag and hurried off.

I stared at the phone again, wondering if I'd misinterpreted. He'd insinuated he'd be wearing something different at the end—did that mean he'd be putting a jacket back on, or...? Or taking something off. Imaginary or not, I'd never been on a date before and flirting was a language I didn't understand. Shit. I was getting in way over my head.

Akari: I was thinking of all the way through?

Linc: You're too damn cute. Okay. Since we're going somewhere classy I better put on a shirt and tie. How about you? I'd like to see you in a dress.

Apart from the long evening dress Holborn required me to wear for performances, which covered me to my feet, I didn't own one and with good reason.

Akari: No, no dress. Trousers. And how about a smile?

Linc: Deal :)

I popped into a quiet corridor to prove that I was, in fact, wearing one now and took a selfie. Within seconds I received a picture back. My smile only grew bigger.

My cheerful mood lasted until I got down the stairs, when I saw the dean beckoning Linc away from his cleaning cart. Bile rose in my throat as I imagined what was about to happen, and I couldn't stop shaking. Then when I glimpsed Jansen out of the corner of my eye, smirking as he watched them walk towards the dean's office, I seriously considered calling Emmy and asking for tips on how to throttle someone.

How could he be so self-obsessed as to try and take over my life like that? Well, he could take his practice and shove it. Furious, I marched out of school, already on the phone to my driver.

"Where are you going?" Jude called after me.

"Home. Can you do me a favour and tell Jansen I hurt my shoulder in yoga?" It was sort of true.

"I'll send him a text. I'm not staying if you're not. He'll make me play until my fingers bleed." He hopped a little. "Come to think of it, maybe I tweaked a hamstring."

"How does that stop you from playing the cello?"

"Good point. Food poisoning ought to do it."

I managed a smile. "Thanks. I'll see you tomorrow."

"Don't forget your flak jacket."

The car was two streets from home when my phone rang.

"Where are you?" Linc asked. "The dean was looking for you."

"Home. I saw him take you away and decided Jansen can practise by himself tonight if it's that important to him."

"Feisty. I like that."

"So what happened?"

He sighed, loud and deep. "The dean accused me of breaking the rules again last night, so I got the buddy I went to the gym with to call and set him straight. His apology wasn't gracious, but it happened."

I let out a long breath. "Thank goodness. I was so worried."

"Don't be. I'm a big boy."

Was he? My hands hadn't reached that low while we were on the bike. "So now what?"

"Right now? Well, I'm done for the day and you're free, so what about lobster, chocolate mousse, shirt, tie and no dress?"

"Are you serious?"

"Why not? If we're going to get blamed for something, we might as well do it."

"You mind if I spend some time with my son first?" The unexpected early finish meant I could feed him and put him to bed myself, rather than Sofia playing mom again.

"Shall I pick you up in two hours?"

"Two hours is perfect." Linc was perfect.

Sofia squealed when I told her I was going out with a man. "On a date?"

"I think so."

"Where's he taking you?"

"I'm not sure. He mentioned lobster and chocolate."

"Definitely a date. Is this with the guy you spoke about the other day? Lincoln?"

I nodded and looked at my feet. "I really like him."

"Aw, this is so great! But you've only got an hour and a half? Go take a shower and I'll help with your hair."

"I don't need to do any of that. He sees me like this

every day. I just want to spend some time with Hisashi and change my blouse."

"Uh, are you sure?" Her expression told me she couldn't contemplate someone going out without a makeover first. Maybe I should get her to spend more time with Bradley?

"Positive." I reached out for my son. "Why don't you take a break?"

By the time Linc's motorcycle engine broke through the peace of the evening, Hisashi was asleep, and I'd given in to Sofia's badgering and sprayed perfume on.

"Stay out as late as you want," she said. "I've got Netflix."

"Thanks," I called, as I dashed down the path into Linc's waiting arms.

He'd never hugged me like that before, but he knew what I needed tonight, and he gave it to me. His heart beat slow and steady in his chest, a contrast to mine which thought it was competing for gold in the 800 metres.

"You ready to go?" he finally asked.

"Yes."

"I bought you a smaller helmet. Here." He passed it over.

Oh shit, he was really serious about this, wasn't he? Why else would he have gone out and spent that much money? Especially when his janitor's salary couldn't be that high. I tugged the helmet on, relieved to find it fitted perfectly, then climbed onto the seat behind him. This time I was prepared for the sensations that washed through me, but it didn't make them any less pleasant. I was almost sorry when after forty minutes we pulled up outside an Italian place in a quiet town in the suburbs.

"Hungry?" he asked, taking my hand as he helped me down.

"Ravenous." And I wouldn't mind something to eat, either.

"I hope you like this place. They do the best pasta, all homemade."

I didn't care about the food, only the company, and even as the waiter leaned in and snapped a napkin over my lap, I barely flinched. A month ago that would have been enough to send me into a panic, but Linc calmed my nerves. I couldn't break my gaze away from him. The flickering candlelight turned his eyes into rippling pools, deep enough to drown in.

"I'll give you a few minutes, sir," the waiter said.

Linc didn't bother to look at the menu. "No need. We'll have lobster with linguine to start with then tiramisu for dessert." He turned to me once the waiter left. "It's not quite chocolate mousse, but it's the closest they have."

"I love tiramisu."

"Then here's to our first date." He poured a glass of white wine and handed it to me before filling his own glass halfway. "Cheers."

We clinked glasses as I tried to put Hisashi's father out of my mind. We'd never had the chance to do this and now we never would, but for my son's sake I needed to try and make something of my life, and the best shot of doing that was sitting in front of me.

Or so I thought.

"Lincoln Macbride?" a man's voice boomed from over my left shoulder. A portly figure stopped next to me and stooped to get a better look. "It is you. Long time, no see."

Linc stuck out his hand and shook with the stranger. "Good to see you, General."

"Akari, this is my old boss, General Thornlow. General, this is my...girlfriend, Akari."

Girlfriend? We hadn't spoken about that. Was he being a little hasty?

"Upgraded the wife, then?" He gave Linc a pat on the back, and he choked on his wine. "Done the same thing myself." The general waved his meaty paw at a petite blonde hovering in the background while I nearly brought up my own drink.

Wife? Linc was married? Why the hell hadn't he mentioned that? Clearly Linc was going through the same thought process because his face drained of colour.

"We got divorced."

"Oh, after the incident?"

"Yes."

"Shame. Still, looks like you've got your act together now, son. You working again?"

"I am."

"Good, good, glad to hear it. Anyway, must dash. These young things take a lot of keeping up with, don't they?" He gave Linc a wink then strode back to his lady friend who'd started inching towards the door.

"Wife, Linc?"

He mouthed an expletive. "I should have told you, I know I should. It's just not an easy thing to bring up in conversation."

"So it was better for me to find out by accident?"

"No, of course not. But I promise you it's over. We split years ago."

"Oh, yes, right. After the 'incident.'" I used my fingers to form quotation marks around the word. "Care to share what that was all about?"

He went rigid, and this time when he looked at me, his eyes were empty. "I'm not so good at talking about it."

I realised I'd crossed a line, and while I couldn't go backwards, I wished I'd trodden more cautiously. "What happened?" I whispered.

Was this another occasion when he thought I deserved the truth? Because if so, I wasn't sure I wanted to hear it. I cringed inside as he began to speak again.

"My squad got ambushed in Afghanistan. Nine men, and six of them died. When the bomb went off, the Taliban started shooting, and I tried to save them, but I couldn't help them all. Never was much good for front line duty after that. I got an honourable discharge."

My fingers scrabbled for his hand and held it tight. "I'm so sorry. I need to learn to stop asking so many questions."

A little life came back into his eyes. "No, you don't. If we're going to make anything of this, it's something you should know."

"Hisashi's father's dead," I blurted. If we were supposed to be telling our secrets, I had to offer mine as well.

"Sweetheart, I'm not sure what to say." He got up and came to my side. "I just figured...I don't know, that you'd split up."

"He was murdered. He tried to make a better life for both of us, and they killed him for it." Tears ran down my cheeks as I gulped in air, and my nose leaked onto Linc's tie. Shit, I was such a mess.

"Shhh, just breathe." He stroked my hair as he held me, and the repetitive motion soothed me a little.

"I ruined our date," I sniffled.

"We both did a good job of that. You want to leave?"

The waiter interrupted. "I have the linguine with the lobster, and a delicious... Shall I come back?"

I sat up, trying to stop my nose from running. "No, it's fine. Just leave it here."

He practically threw the dishes onto the table and beat a hasty retreat.

"You sure you want to eat?" Linc asked.

"Y-y-you said you'd feed me lobster."

"Then I will, sweetheart."

I calmed down enough to eat, although I couldn't manage more than a few bites of tiramisu. At least I hadn't taken Sofia's advice and worn mascara, or the situation would have been a whole lot worse. Even so, I felt drained as Linc tucked his jacket round my shoulders and led me from the restaurant.

"You okay to ride back? I can call a cab if you're tired."

"But then your bike would be here. How would you get to work?"

"Doesn't matter. I'll sort something out."

"No, I'll ride back. I'm fine."

"I'll take it slow."

Four words every woman liked to hear, but I wished the circumstances were different. I climbed up behind him and clung on as he navigated his way through the quiet streets, arriving at my apartment just before midnight.

"Shall I walk you up?"

"No, it's okay. I'll sneak in. I don't want to wake the others."

He took both my hands in his and pulled me closer. "Thank you for coming with me tonight."

"I wrecked it."

"Those things needed to be said."

"It doesn't make it hurt any less."

"I know. All we can do is try to replace the bad memories with good ones." A shiver ran through me as he leaned down and brushed his lips softly over the corner of my mouth. "I want to make a lot of memories with you."

With those words, he managed to turn darkness into dawn, night into day. I smiled as I pressed against him. The idea of making memories with Linc made my insides smoulder with things I hadn't thought about in years.

"We can't forget the past," I whispered, my face smushed into his chest. "But let's live for the future."

CHAPTER 18

"LEFT A BIT. A bit more. Stop!" Bradley spoke into a walkie talkie as my new Fazioli swung in mid-air above the roof terrace on Saturday morning.

I forced myself to unclench my teeth and said a silent prayer the crane driver knew what he was doing. Was it supposed to tilt like that?

I breathed a sigh of relief as the wheels touched down into the waiting cradle, and a team of specialist movers sprang forward to manoeuvre the piano into its new home in the lounge.

"Thanks so much for sorting this out," I said to Bradley, as he brushed a piece of imaginary dirt off his epaulettes. He'd gone for the army look today, although the only place he'd be camouflaged was in a flock of flamingos. And not many four-star generals tended to accessorise with sparkly purple boots, either.

"No problem, chicky. I wasn't about to leave you to organise this crew yourself. They already tried to delay the delivery twice."

"Are you staying for dinner?"

"No can do. Emmy's having a wardrobe crisis, and I have to fly to Paris and sort it out."

Given that Emmy would happily live in jeans if she could get away with it, I suspected it was actually Bradley who was having the crisis on her behalf. "It was lovely to see you."

"I'm glad you're smiling. We were a bit worried about you moving here by yourself."

"I'm making friends."

"Super. And you..." He turned to Sofia. "Lovely to see you again. I'll get Emmy's housekeeper to send those recipes over."

When I'd walked in on them chatting in the kitchen earlier, Sofia mentioned something about ice cream, and I recalled the freezer full of delights at Emmy's house. Bradley volunteered her to have a go at recreating some of them.

Bouncing Hisashi on my hip, we all walked to the door to wave Bradley off, skirting around the huge pile of gifts he'd brought with him. It took the driver four trips to carry them upstairs, and by the end he'd been muttering about hiring another crane.

"It's finally here. I can't believe it," I said, when we walked back into the lounge.

The shiny wood felt cool under my fingertips, and I sat down with Hisashi on my lap and played a few notes. Not Brahms or Schubert. Jansen had tainted those. I chose Beethoven's Moonlight Sonata, at least until Hisashi joined in, pushing his little fingers on the keys.

Sofia stopped to listen. "Wow, you're good. Awesome to finally have your own piano, right?"

"I'm so relieved it's arrived."

"Does this mean you'll come home earlier in the evenings?"

"I'll have to do some practice for the recitals with Jude and Jansen, but I'm going to try and get home early three days a week." Of course, I hadn't told

Jansen that yet, and I couldn't see him giving in without a fight. But since I'd spent time with Linc, he'd allowed me to find a strength hidden away inside myself that I didn't know existed, and I was determined to stand up to Jansen for the sake of my son.

"That's great. And Bradley's right—it's good to see you smiling. I get the feeling that isn't all down to the piano, though?"

Sofia had gone out for a late bowling session with friends as soon as I got back last night, so we hadn't had a chance to catch up since my near-disaster of a date. "You're right. Linc's also helped with that."

"So tell me all the juicy details."

I cringed a little bit inside, unused to spilling my private life. But this was what girls were supposed to do, right?

"Uh, well it went a bit wrong at first. I found out he was married."

Her eyes went wide. "No way! Married? Wait, is he divorced now? Or messing you around?"

"He's divorced. And he was in the army and some horrible things happened to him in Afghanistan." I didn't want to go into too much detail—it was his story to tell, not mine. I'd only told Sofia the bare bones of what happened to me, and I knew how important privacy could be.

"Sounds like you had a hoot. Did it get any better?"

"He got upset, I got upset, then he fed me tiramisu and acted really sweet. And he brought me home, and when we stopped outside he...kissed me." I finished on a whisper and felt myself blush.

"Tongues?"

Had she turned into Emmy? That's exactly what she

would have asked. "No! Just...he's got really soft lips."

"Well at least that made up for things. When's he taking you out again?"

"I don't know, or even if he is. He didn't say anything." And when I messaged him yesterday morning to find out how he was, I got a text back saying he'd had to leave town unexpectedly, and he'd call me when he got back. Was that a brush off? My heart seized at the thought.

"You didn't ask?"

"Well, no. You think I should have?"

"He brought you back and kissed you, after a date that sounds like it floated on the edge of calamity. He's probably as nervous as you are about the prospects for a second."

"But what if I ask him and he says no?"

She shrugged. "You can't win them all, but if you don't play the game the only thing certain is that you'll lose."

Something about the way she said that, nonchalant but with a quake in her voice, told me she'd played and lost at some point in her life. But I tamped down my curiosity, refusing to pry because I didn't want to invite more questions on my own past.

Besides, she was right. If he didn't call, I'd have to pick up the phone. The thought terrified me.

The Fazioli played like a dream, so crisp and clear it made the school's pianos sound as if they'd been picked up cheap at a garage sale. Even more reason to practise at home.

Now I just had to break the news to Jansen—another conversation I didn't want to have.

I saw him in class on Monday morning, as we went over our recital pieces with Dr. Vasilyevich, but at that point I still hadn't worked out what to say.

I was still stewing over it in the voice seminar before lunch, thankfully one that Il Duce didn't share. Instead, I sat next to Jude as he showed once again that he had a surprisingly good singing voice. Secretly, I believed he had more talent than Jansen, he simply didn't like to work as much.

"You want to get lunch with me after this?" he asked, as we left the seminar room.

"You don't have a hot date today?" While listening for rumours circulating about Linc and me, I couldn't help hearing tales of Jude's efforts to bed every eligible female in Boston.

"I'm between girls at the moment."

"Since when?"

"Since I snuck out of Maria's apartment this morning. Or was it Martina?"

"You're impossible, you know that?"

He grinned, displaying dimples that would have had more of an effect if Linc hadn't gotten under my skin already.

"But you still like me. Besides, it'll take some of the heat off you and loverboy."

Okay, I did still like him. It was difficult not to. And he had a point about taking attention away from Linc. I tried to inject a little enthusiasm into my voice. "Great, let's get lunch."

The chef must have been on a health kick, because the serving counters groaned under the weight of quinoa, spinach, beetroot, and salmon, and every dessert was topped with blueberries.

"What are these?" Jude peered at one of the dishes.

"Sweet potato fries, I think."

"Ugh. What's wrong with normal fries? I'm a growing man. I need to keep my strength up."

Still, he piled his plate high as I opted for a salad. I'd found my strength in Linc. We found a quiet table in one corner, and I settled into my seat as Jude popped a couple of fries into his mouth.

"Hmm. Not bad. I could get used to these. And all this health food means I can have an extra beer tonight."

"Tonight? We have practice tonight."

He rubbed his temple as his forehead creased into an exaggerated frown. "I've got a headache."

"You mean you're not going?"

"Jansen's an arsehole. Nobody needs to practice the same piece ten hours a week, not for a school recital. We'll all go stale."

"He doesn't see it that way."

"He doesn't see anything but himself. I heard he's riding roughshod over his violin group as well. Three of them are supposed to be composing a piece, but he's written it all himself and it's terrible."

"At least it's not just us."

"Nah, don't take it personally."

"I try, but sometimes it's difficult. Uh, I'm not planning to go tonight either."

Jude hooted with laughter, and I shushed him as the girls on the next table stared at us. "Brilliant. He can practice by himself to his heart's content."

"How do we tell him?"

"He'll get the message when we don't show up."

"I can't do that! It's rude."

Jude shrugged. "So? He doesn't deserve courtesy. I might send him a text message if I get round to it."

"I don't want to speak to him. Maybe I could leave a note?"

"If you want." He leaned in a bit closer. "You going out with the janitor guy tonight?"

I choked on a forkful of shredded spinach. "Uh, I'm not sure, I mean..."

"Yeah, you are. Don't worry, I won't tell anyone. It's a stupid rule anyway. I shag the girl who cleans my room every Thursday before class, like that's gonna get me a better grade."

"Really?"

He shook his head. "I don't need better grades anyway. Believe it or not, I always get decent passes."

"I meant about the girl." How could he drop that into conversation so casually?

His dimples popped out again. "Got to limber myself up for those sodding yoga lessons. Look, if you get pulled in by the dean again, just tell him you were with me. I'll back you up."

That may not do much for my own reputation, but despite his philandering ways, Jude knew how to be sweet. "That's kind of you to offer."

"What are friends for?"

An hour before Jansen was due to arrive, I snuck into the practice room, pen and notepad in hand. I had a small pile of balled-up attempts in front of me when I heard footsteps at the door.

"Starting early?" Linc asked.

"I didn't realise you'd come back."

"I only flew in an hour ago. Thought I'd better come in and sort out my schedule with the maintenance supervisor so I know what else I can fit around it this week."

"Do you mean me?" I whispered.

He stepped into the room and pushed the door closed. "Yeah, I mean you. I missed you like crazy."

"I thought I might have scared you off."

"Never." He reached out a hand then glanced at the door and thought the better of it. "My godson had an accident, fell out of a treehouse and broke his leg. His momma freaked out, so I needed to go and give her a hand."

"You have a godson?"

"Braydon. He's eight, and he lives in Springfield. His daddy was in the army with me."

"Was? Did he...?"

"He was one of my squad in Afghanistan, and he didn't make it back."

"I really wish I could hug you right now."

His half-smile was better than none at all. "I'd like nothing more than to hold you in my arms, but Il Duce is probably hovering outside with a camera. What time are you done tonight?"

"Right as soon as I can write this note to Jansen telling him my piano's arrived and I'll be practising at home on Mondays, Wednesdays and Fridays."

Now I got a proper smile. "My week suddenly got better."

"Except I can't decide what to write, and I'm still

not sure leaving a note's the best idea. Do you think I should stay and talk to him?"

"There's an old Irish proverb that says 'a good retreat is better than a bad stand.'"

"A note it is, then." I scribbled some more then held it up for Linc to read. "Is that okay?"

"You've apologised three times in the first sentence."

"Maybe I'll take the last 'sorry' out."

"Take them all out."

"You're sure?"

"You haven't done anything wrong. I checked the room bookings, and none of the other groups are rehearsing more than twice a week."

I had another go, removing all the apologies. "Better?"

"Better. Now, do you want to get something to eat later?"

CHAPTER 19

WHEN LINC ASKED me where I wanted to meet, I'd hesitated. We couldn't go anywhere someone from school might see us, but I didn't want to invite him over to my apartment. Meeting my son would be a big step, and it was too soon. I needed to get to know Linc better first. After the surprises I'd had on our first date, I couldn't help wondering what else lurked under the surface.

"I don't know the area very well. Maybe a coffee shop, or somewhere else we can get a bite to eat?"

"I know a place. I'll pick you up outside your place at eight?"

"Okay."

Now I was waiting in the lobby, listening for Linc's bike. The evenings were already getting colder, and if this kept up I'd have to consider buying a leather jacket.

A roar sounded in the distance, and I stepped outside. That was another problem—with Linc's bike there was no sneaking around.

He unstrapped my helmet from the back seat, but before I could put it on he leaned over and pressed his lips to mine.

"Missed you," he said.

My skin burned where he touched me, but only in a

good way. "You only saw me three hours ago."

"That's still too long."

I climbed onto the bike behind him, tucking my hands into his front pockets to keep warm. I needed to add gloves to my shopping list as well. "Where are we going?"

"I know a family who runs a restaurant near here. We can borrow the room at the back for an hour. I hope you like Chinese food."

"It just became my new favourite thing."

When I tried the array of dishes that arrived at the table soon after we did, I found I'd been telling the truth. "This is amazing. What is it?"

The old lady who served us laughed as she shook her head. "Ah, is secret recipe. My mother taught it to me. Is Mr. Lincoln's favourite."

He nodded in agreement. "She's not kidding. I could live on the stuff. Every time I came home this was the first meal I'd eat."

"I might just become a regular customer myself."

Every other dish tasted delicious, too, but with the restaurant owner bustling around like Linc was her long-lost son, we didn't get much beyond small talk. Every time we tried to turn the conversation to a more serious topic, she interrupted with a question or comment.

"It so nice to see that Mr. Lincoln has a girl. You come back soon?"

"We will, I promise." Linc bent to peck her on the cheek, and I felt an irrational sense of jealousy. Crazy, because she was old enough to be his grandmother, but I wanted those lips to myself.

"Well, that was the most excruciating experience of

my life," he said, as we walked back to the bike.

"She meant well."

He grimaced. "I felt like a spare part on my own date. I thought she was going to invite herself back for coffee."

"She probably has a special recipe for that."

On the way back, the weather gods conspired against us too, as big, fat drops of rain started to fall. Linc slowed down as the road surface got more slippery, and by the time he pulled up outside my apartment I was soaked through.

"Go inside before you catch a chill," he said, leaving the bike idling as we both pulled our helmets off.

"But..."

"Don't want you sick, sweetheart."

On impulse, I leaned down and kissed him. I'd meant to be brief, but he grabbed my butt with both hands, tipped me into him then followed it up with a swipe of his tongue. Then as quick as he started, he stopped. I tried to capture his lips again, but he let go and took a step back.

"Good to see I'm not the only one with needs." He chuckled. "Now go get dry. I'll see you Wednesday."

"I can't wait," I whispered, and this time I managed to meet his eyes.

Even the rain couldn't dampen my spirits as I skipped up the path, but as I got inside a cold dose of reality hit. I wanted this man, but my scars were physical as well as mental. What would he say if he saw all of me? Or would I be too scared to find out?

On Wednesday, I still didn't have the answer, but I did have a new sweater, a maroon one with a hood, and I wore it pulled low over my eyes as I snuck out of school past the cameras. Jansen walked down the corridor in front of me, and I turned away from him as well. I'd already had a tongue-lashing from him yesterday, and not the pleasant kind. That I hoped to get from Linc later, if I managed to make it through the car park without being seen. In mid-afternoon, the campus was still full of students and worse, faculty members, but my classes were done for the day, Linc had the early shift, and we didn't want to waste any time we could spend together.

I ran the last few steps to his bike, which was purring away, ready to go. As soon as I swung my leg over the back, I yanked the helmet on and buckled it up. "Go."

We were heading for a pizza place near the park, far enough from school that students didn't make a habit of eating there. As the fellows tended towards three courses with wine, we figured they wouldn't go there either. We wanted a bit of alone time without getting interrupted.

That seemed like a good plan until we got to dessert. The menu didn't have chocolate mousse, but ice cream ran a close second. As Linc raised the spoon to my mouth, a shadow fell over the table, and we looked up to see the percussion teacher looming.

"Well, well, well. I though you two weren't supposed to be together?"

Oh shit, shit, shit. Beads of sweat popped out and ran down my spine, a chilling reminder of the lecture from the dean. I opened my mouth then realised I had absolutely no idea what to say. Staring at the table felt like a good option, but I couldn't let Linc take the blame for this so I forced my head up.

Only he looked remarkably calm. "Maybe not, but what would your wife think of your little tête-à-tête with the dean's secretary?"

"We're here for a business meeting."

"Really? I've never had a colleague rub their foot in my crotch before. That a new thing?"

I almost choked on my tongue, but Linc squeezed my hand under the table and that kept me calm.

The percussion teacher went a shade redder. "I don't know what you're talking about."

Linc shrugged and looked straight at him. "And the other day when you had a 'meeting' in your car at lunchtime, I presume she'd lost her contact lens in your lap?"

"You were watching? You... You filthy pervert."

"Hard not to catch an eyeful when the path to the tool shed runs right alongside that parking space. If you hadn't been focused on what she was doing with her mouth, maybe you'd have noticed?"

"You're disgusting." The man sneered at us. "I'm not the only one keeping an eye on you. It's just a matter of time."

He marched off, and Linc slid off his seat and crouched beside me. "Sweetheart, you're shaking. It's okay. He can't touch us."

"But what about the next person who sees? You have dirt on all of them?" Hisashi's father once told me blackmail was an art form. He'd been proficient at it, and Emmy was the master, but I couldn't keep running to her for help. Linc and I needed to fight this battle, but how?

"Sadly not. We got lucky today. We'll have to be more careful next time."

Lucky today? Surely he meant unlucky? "What are we supposed to do? Wear bags over our heads? Go for dinner in the next state?"

"How about I make dinner on Friday? There's no prying eyes in my kitchen, and I've got a couch for canoodling on."

"Canoodling?" I'd worked hard on my English, but I hadn't heard that word before.

"Making out."

Oh. Oh! "I think I'll like canoodling. But can you cook?"

"I can dial."

"It's a date then."

On Friday morning, the thought of spending a whole evening with Linc meant even Jansen's nitpicking went over my head. At least until lunchtime. Then the nerves kicked in so badly I couldn't eat. I was going to spend a whole evening with Linc. Alone.

I'd felt guilty about leaving Hisashi, but he hadn't wanted his afternoon nap today, and by the time Sofia shoved me out the apartment he was already fast asleep.

"We'll be fine. Don't worry." She grinned wide enough for both of us. "And I don't expect you to come home early, either."

But I still felt nervous. Linc knew something was up as soon as I walked out of the building. His forehead creased into a frown, and by the time I reached him he'd got off the bike and held out his arms.

"What's wrong, sweetheart?"

"Nothing."

He leaned back and stared at me.

"Okay, but it's silly."

"Try me."

"I've never done the whole dating thing. Obviously I have been alone with a man before, but that was...different. I don't know what you expect."

"What I expect..." He dropped his arms and took my hand instead. "Is for you to eat the Chinese I've lovingly ordered, pick a movie you want to watch, laugh in the appropriate places, and enjoy yourself."

"But what about the canoodling?" My cheeks heated, and I couldn't look him in the eye.

"I'm not going to say no, but I'll leave it up to you."

I let out the breath I'd been holding, and all my pent up fears flooded out with it. "Thank you."

He held out my helmet. "Are you ready to go now?"

Definitely.

Curiosity got the better of me as Linc drove. Apart from saying it was on the other side of town, he'd barely mentioned anything about his apartment. Would it be homey or a man-cave? Was he messy or neat? On his salary, it was probably small, but beyond that I really didn't know what to expect.

Half an hour later, he slowed outside a three-storey building and turned down a narrow alley. It was dimly lit by a single yellowed street lamp, and once my eyes adjusted I made out the shadows of refuse bins and a few beaten-up cars. He parked next to one of them and helped me off the bike.

"Not as swanky as your place," he said, apologetically.

If only he'd seen the shithole I lived in before—a sweaty, miserable hovel where the water ran brown and mosquitoes kept me company. "I don't care."

On the second floor, he pushed open the door at the end of the hallway and flicked on the light, motioning me through in front of him. The delicious smell of something chocolatey wafted out.

"Is that dessert? Can we skip dinner?"

"I baked cookies."

"Really?"

"I used ready-to-bake dough from the store, so at least they'll be edible. And no, you can wait. Dinner will be here in a couple of minutes."

I pouted but it was no good, he wouldn't give in. Although when the food arrived and I realised it was the special-recipe chicken we had the other night I was kind of glad about that.

"I'll set the table." Might as well make myself useful. "Where do you keep the plates?"

"Um, try that cupboard over there." He pointed next to the sink.

"Nope. This is cleaning stuff. You don't know where you keep the plates?"

"Usually I just eat out of the cartons."

My eyes rolled all of their own accord, and I opened and closed cupboards until I found an assortment of dishes. "Spoons? Can you remember where those are?"

"There's always chopsticks in the bag."

Eventually I got the table in the corner of the living room set for two, having shoved a pile of bodybuilding magazines and a stray baseball cap onto the floor.

"What's that?" I pointed at one of the chairs. "That metal thing?"

"Oh, it's the gear lever off my old bike. Probably I could get rid of it."

I had some work to do here. Domesticating Linc looked to be a challenge. What on earth would he do if takeaways didn't exist? Starve? But I couldn't complain because dinner was delicious, and I loaded the dishwasher while Linc bagged up the trash. "Do you have any dishwasher tablets?"

He shrugged. Yes, definitely needed work.

When he came back in, I'd wiped down the surfaces in the kitchen, and he took the cloth out of my hand.

"I didn't ask you here to clean."

"I don't mind."

Although the therapist's words flitted through my mind. *You're acclimated to slavery*, she'd told me. I tried to block those thoughts. What was wrong with looking after Linc? After all, I cared about him.

He interrupted my runaway brain. "Well, I do mind. I've got other plans for you."

Ah yes, the canoodling. "Is it movie time?"

"Why don't you pick something while I open a bottle of wine? The DVDs are in the rack by the TV."

The rack held a bewildering array. *Frozen*? *The Lion King*? I'd never have put Linc down as a Disney fan. *Die Hard*, now that was more like it. Hang on, what was this? *Pulp Friction*? *Lord of the G-Strings*? I was still holding a dubious copy of *Free Willy* that definitely wasn't PG rated when he walked into the room.

"What do you want to watch?" he asked.

"Uh..."

He came closer and peered at what I was holding. "What the hell?"

"I think that's my question."

"That's not mine, I swear. I let a buddy borrow the apartment while I was away a few months ago, and he must have left it here."

"Them. Left them." I pointed at the other delights in the bottom shelf.

"I'll kill him." He grabbed them all and dumped them in the trash. Was he telling the truth? Or did he have a secret fetish for girl-on-girl action?

"Should I disinfect my fingers?"

"Probably." His disgusted look said he shared my sentiments. "I'm never lending the place to him again, that's for sure. Look, how about Star Wars? I've got the whole set."

"That's some space thing, right?"

"Some space thing? Seriously, you've never seen any of them? Not one?"

"I didn't even have a TV until last year."

I'd binge watched films while living with Emmy, but nobody in her household was a sci-fi fan. At Riverley, movie nights meant guns, explosions, and gore. Everyone picked apart the plots while munching their bodyweight in popcorn and downing beer from the micro-brewery they'd recently clubbed together to buy. Apart from Bradley. Bradley watched musicals and cartoons, and knew every word in *The Devil Wears Prada* by heart.

Linc slung an arm around my shoulders and took

the box containing *Star Wars: Episode 1* from the shelf. "Come, young Padawan. I can see I need to educate you."

The ships were interesting and everything, but my attention was captured by the steady rise and fall of Linc's chest as I leaned against it. His warm breath curled around my ear, and I totally lost track of the plot. An hour passed and all I could think of was the muscular arms wrapped around me and how safe they made me feel.

"Enjoying the film?" Linc asked.

"Yes. It's fantastic."

"Who do think's going to win? The Lakers or the Red Sox?"

"Uh, the Lakers?"

"You're not watching this at all, are you?"

Shit. "Not exactly. I'm distracted."

His voice took on a playful tone. "By what?"

"By stuff."

"What kind of stuff?"

"Okay, fine. You. I'm distracted by you."

"Do you want me to distract you a little more, so you can forget the film entirely?"

I nodded and held my breath. What did he have in mind?

He slid down on the leather sofa, swinging his legs up so I lay on top of him. Then he kissed me, and it wasn't some soft, gentle effort like before. This was a nerve tingling clash of tongues and teeth, and I couldn't get enough of it. He still tasted of cookies—sweet, delicious and so good I wanted to eat the whole plateful. By the time we came up for air, I'd dissolved into a puddle of mush, and the closing credits were almost finished.

"Didn't you say you needed to get home at a sensible time?" he asked.

Probably, but I wished I hadn't. Did three or four o'clock in the morning count?

"Something about your nanny having to go out early?" he prompted.

Oh, yes. "She needs to leave early to stay with her cousin for the weekend."

"I'd better get you home, then."

"I guess."

He leaned up and kissed me again. "I wish I didn't have to either, but you can't leave the girl in the lurch. We'll have plenty more evenings like this."

That night, as I floated up the path to the front door, I felt like doing cartwheels.

CHAPTER 20

OVER THE NEXT two weeks, we settled into a routine. Saturdays were reserved for girl time with Sofia, Jansen and Jude got me for practice on Tuesdays and Thursdays, and I ate dinner with Linc on Wednesdays and Fridays. The rest of the time, when I wasn't in class, I spent with Hisashi, or playing the Fazioli at home. Or texting, emailing and calling Linc while considering whether it was worthwhile buying shares in a telecoms company.

The second recital came and went, and this time I played without missing a note. Linc kept out of the way which disappointed me, but when he brought me a huge bunch of flowers afterwards I couldn't be too upset.

The schedule worked well until Mozart played one Friday afternoon as I left my final music theory class of the week. When I picked up, Sofia sounded frantic.

"My cousin just called. She's had a couple of giddy spells, and they want to keep her in the hospital for tests. Is there any chance I can leave early today so I can look after Jemima?"

Sofia had told me plenty about Jemima, her cousin's four-year-old girl, who by all accounts got herself into huge amounts of trouble by her innate curiosity. Only last week she managed to bring a snail to the dinner table and insisted on giving it a plate of lettuce leaves to munch through while she ate. I still had those joys to come with Hisashi. Maybe I could convince him he'd like a goldfish instead?

"Of course. I'm on my way home, so I should be there by the time you've packed a bag."

"Thanks so much. I'll make it up to you, I promise."

She had nothing to make up, seeing as she put in so many extra hours without complaint, but I couldn't help being disappointed by the prospect of cancelling date night. Linc had been threatening to cook for ages, and tonight he was supposed to be attempting spaghetti bolognese.

I picked up the phone to reschedule, but when he answered that wasn't what came out.

"Sofia's had to go out unexpectedly."

"Sofia? That's your nanny's name?"

"Did I never mention that? Yes, it is. Anyway, I need to postpone."

"Are you sure about Sofia? Or are you just using her as a convenient excuse to avoid my cooking?"

"No, I was looking forward to it, honestly."

"Will you be free tomorrow?"

"She'll be gone the whole weekend." And I'd be lonely. "Look, why don't you come over to my place? It's about time you met Hisashi."

"Really? You're sure you're okay with that?"

No, but I needed to see how he behaved around my son. Linc was now the second biggest piece in my life after Hisashi, and I had to find out how they fitted together. "I'll be home in half an hour, so come over when you're ready. Apartment 404."

Linc turned up at quarter to six carrying a bag of ingredients. I'd found time for a quick tidy up, but Sofia kept the place so neat there wasn't a lot that needed to be done. Once he'd spread out all the meat, spaghetti and vegetables on the counter, I led him through to the lounge where Hisashi was bouncing in his chair.

"This is my son," I said needlessly, picking him up so Linc could see him properly.

Linc held out his arms. "Can I hold him? I promise I won't drop him. I had plenty of practice with my godson."

I didn't know how Hisashi would react, but I stepped closer and passed him over. First he scowled, then giggled and made a grab for Linc's beard.

"Occupational hazard," he said, uncurling Hisashi's tiny fingers.

"Do you want me to take him back?"

"No, we're good here."

And they were. Hisashi cried when the bodyguards held him, and when Emmy or his uncle picked him up he stared at them without making a sound. But Linc soon had him laughing, and they played until my grumbling stomach reminded us about dinner.

"I'll put him to bed," I said. "You're sure you know what you're doing?"

"I printed a recipe off the internet."

"Well, okay then."

Half an hour later, a hideous screeching assaulted my ears, and Hisashi, who'd been on the verge of drifting off, started to scream. I closed his door to keep the noise out and rushed through to the kitchen, where Linc was taking the batteries out of the smoke alarm.

"What happened?"

"I don't know. It smells pretty bad though."

Bad, yes. And plasticky. "What did you put in the oven?"

"Garlic bread."

I peered through the glass window at the melting mess on the tray. "You didn't take it out of the wrapping?"

Blank look. "I had to do that? It just said warm at two hundred degrees."

"Yes, without the plastic bag on it."

"Oh, hell. I ruined it."

I grabbed a tea towel and carried the smoking disaster out to the roof terrace. "It doesn't matter. Just sort out the pasta while I get Hisashi back to sleep."

Dinner turned out surprisingly edible, and Linc even brought chocolate mousse for dessert. Chocolatey goodness and a delicious man to feed it to me—Friday nights didn't get much better.

"Movie?" he asked, after we'd cleared the table.

I nodded, even though we both knew we had no intention of watching it. Canoodling practice took precedence, and I reckoned I was making a definite improvement. Without a peep from the baby monitor on the table next to us, I could put in some serious effort.

Before we knew it, midnight struck, along with a fork of lightning in the sky outside. From the full-length windows in front of the roof terrace, the electrical storm was mesmerising.

"You can't go home in that," I told Linc. "I've got

two spare rooms." Part of me wanted to invite him into mine, but when I thought of the hurdles I still needed to overcome in my own mind, I realised it was too soon.

"You sure?"

"Stay, please."

So he did. For all of Saturday and most of Sunday. As I watched him play with Hisashi through the open kitchen door while I made breakfast, the F-word popped into my mind. Family.

Did I dare to hope for that with Linc? Or was I wishing for something never destined to happen?

CHAPTER 21

TUESDAY EVENING CAME and brought with it a cold. I hadn't felt well during dinner with Linc the evening before, but he'd bundled me up in a blanket and fed me chicken soup, and by the end of the evening I'd been feeling a little better.

Now, my head pounded at the prospect of a practice with Jansen, and I didn't see how I could get through two hours without my nose dribbling all over the keys. A delightful prospect.

Linc: Tell him you're sick.

Akari: But he'll make me stay tomorrow instead and I'd rather be with you.

Linc: I'd rather you were with me too, but I want you to get better more than anything.

Akari: I'll be okay. I've taken that medicine you gave me.

Linc: If you're sure, but the instant you feel worse, go home.

Akari: Miss you x.

Linc: Miss you too x.

I'd lied. I didn't feel okay. I also felt guilty for telling Linc I felt okay, but there were some times when a little fib was better for everybody, right?

By the fourth run through Beethoven's Piano Trio No. 3, my wrists ached, and I could only breathe from one side of my nose.

"Would you stop that noise?" Jansen asked. He'd been tetchy since we got in there. Maybe he forgot to take his meds.

"What noise?"

"That disgusting sniffling."

I tried to clear my nose quietly, but a tickle in my throat set off a coughing fit.

"And the coughing, too. We don't want your germs."

That did it. "You know what? I'm going home. I feel like shit, so you might as well carry on without me." I shoved the stool back and got shakily to my feet, but Jansen planted himself in front of me.

"No, you'll stay. I've got the room booked until eight."

"I'll puke by seven thirty."

He shoved me back, and I fell on the stool again. "Then do it quietly."

"Don't talk to her like that." Jude came up behind him, eyes narrowed.

"You can shut up as well. You clearly haven't practiced since last week, so you need all the help you can get."

"I damn well have. I spent three hours in here yesterday."

"When? Because I was here for six."

I got to my feet again. "I'm going home."

Jansen whirled round to face me again, but this time he kept pushing until he had me pinned against the wall. "Back to the janitor, more like. I know you're still slumming it with him."

As Jansen bore down on me with his weight, fears

I'd kept locked away broke free, followed by the instincts I'd had to live on. There was a satisfying "oof" as my knee connected with his gonads.

Hisashi's father taught me how to do that, in case I got bothered by the guards again. "You kick, you run, you come to me, *querida*. I'll deal with it." I still remembered his soft voice as he instructed me on the best spot to aim for, a technique Emmy helped me to perfect a couple of years later.

Jude stared open mouthed as I ran past them both, my only thought to get away. The slap of my feet on the tiles echoed through the corridors as I bolted for the front door.

I shot into the darkness, not knowing or caring where I was going. I didn't stop until I ran out of breath, and by then I'd reached the park three blocks away. The moonlight reflected off ripples in the duck pond as I gulped in air, tears mixing with snot. I wiped my face with a sleeve, thankful Linc wasn't there to see me in such a state.

Except he knew. My phone played the opening beats of "Bohemian Rhapsody," and I fished it out of my pocket. At least it wasn't "Killer Queen." Trying to explain this mess to Emmy would be even worse.

"Sweetheart, where are you?"

"T-t-the park."

"Stay where you are; I'll be there in five."

I sank onto a bench and stared at the shadows cast by the branches overhead. A lone duck waddled out to stare at me, no doubt wondering who this intruder was in his peaceful paradise. Must be nice to be a duck. Nothing to do all day but swim around, eat bread, and...

"What the hell happened?" Linc's voice startled me.

I stood up beside him, staring out into the trees. "Jansen was being an ass. Nothing new, except I didn't feel up to dealing with him tonight."

"You had me terrified, running out like that."

"How did you know?"

"I bumped into Jude in the lobby. He was looking for you as well."

"He tried to stick up for me, but Jansen had a go at him too."

"Jansen needs to be taught a lesson." Linc's hands balled into fists, and his eyes flashed with anger.

"No, don't. Don't lower yourself to his level. He's not normally this bad."

"He upsets you every week."

"I need to learn to toughen up."

"No, you don't. You're perfect as you are. Don't ever lose that sweetness."

"I've always dreamed of being able to stand up for myself, but when I tried it tonight it was harder than I'd ever imagined." How did Emmy do it? She'd never have let Jansen get the better of her like that. Some people might call her a bitch, but she only looked after herself and everyone she cared about.

"We'll work on that. It just takes practice."

He took my hands and fireworks went off. No, literally. On the far side of the pond, starbursts of green and gold lit up the night sky, the lights sizzling as they twinkled back to earth. A series of bangs brought explosions of red and pink, and I stopped to watch for a few seconds. I hadn't seen a display since Bradley arranged World War III in Emmy's backyard last Christmas.

I squeezed Linc's hand, and he gripped mine back tighter. And tighter. And tighter.

"Linc, you're hurting me. Could you...? What's wrong?" His eyes were closed and sweat popped out on his brow as he started shaking uncontrollably. "Linc, you're scaring me. What's wrong with you?"

He collapsed onto the bench I'd been sitting on, gasping for breath, eyes screwed up like he was in pain.

"Linc!" My voice rose to a near shriek. "What's happening?"

He clutched at my cheeks, cupping them in his hands and squeezing them together. "Don't leave me. Don't go. Please. Don't leave me."

I watched in horror as his tears fell and used my clean sleeve to wipe them away. Why was he so scared? I looked around, but I couldn't see anything, and the fireworks meant my hearing was useless as well. Then it struck me. That damned noise. He'd been in a war, and that ended in trauma. Was he having a panic attack? After I'd got to America I'd had several myself, triggered by reminders of my last hours in Colombia. Smoke. Screams. The crackle of flames. When I got that choking feeling, I barely recognized my surroundings. Instead, I flew right back to the hell of the jungle. My episodes had eased after I moved back to Japan, but I still remembered the fear vividly.

"Don't go. Please don't go." Linc's plea, so plaintive, cut through to my core.

I tried to move my hand to relieve the pain of him squeezing it then clasped my other one over the top. "I'm here. I'm not going anywhere, I promise." Without knowing what else to do, I climbed onto his lap and wrapped my free arm around his head, trying to cover his ears and block out the noise. My heart beat faster as I clung to him, praying for an end to the nightmare. "I'm staying."

He gulped air faster as he buried his head in my shoulder. That *damned* noise. The fireworks seemed to last forever, and after they'd finally subsided another minute went by before Linc looked up and opened his eyes again. By then, my heart was racing as quickly as his.

It took a few seconds for him to focus on me. "Fuck, sweetheart, are you okay?"

"Am I okay? I'm not the one who just had a panic attack. That's what it was, isn't it?"

He loosened his grip on my hand and brought it to his lips before nodding. "PTSD. I thought it was getting better. I haven't had an attack in months, but that one caught me by surprise."

"You and me both."

With the sky quiet once more, we sat in silence for a few minutes, until our breathing returned to normal.

"Every time I hear a loud bang, it takes me back to that road in Afghanistan. The explosion, the shooting, the death. I carried my best friend for half a mile, holding his guts in with one hand while I shot at enemy soldiers with the other. He died in my arms."

Now it was my turn to cry, as he stared into the void behind me. Not for myself, but for Linc's friend, lost in battle, for Hisashi's father, and all the other people lost in the Colombian nightmare I'd escaped.

"Horrible things happen to good people, Linc. I used to ask myself why, but then I realised it's human nature. Some people are born screwed in the head, some are made that way. All we can do is fight against it whatever way we can, in the hope that one day the world will be at peace." I hugged him harder. "But in the meantime, let's try to find peace together."

"So fucking sweet. I don't know who sent you to me, but I thank my lucky stars every day that they did."

Sofia was stretched out on the sofa in the lounge when I walked in with Linc, and she did a double take to see him behind me.

"Sofia, this is Linc. Linc, this is Sofia."

For a few seconds she frowned, but then her face cleared and her usual smile returned. "Lovely to meet you. Can I get you something to drink?"

Linc hesitated, so I replied for both of us. "It's been a long day, so I think we'll just go to bed."

"You know what? You're right. I'll do the same." She picked her magazine and the baby monitor off the coffee table and headed first to Hisashi's room then a few seconds later to her own.

Sofia's hasty departure spared me from having to keep my eyes open any longer, and for that my fuzzy head was grateful. Linc yawned, and I could tell the evening's events had taken their toll. "I hope you weren't kidding about bed. I feel like I could sleep for a week."

"Same." I paused. "Linc?"

"Yes?"

"Will you stay with me tonight? Not to...you know. Just to be there."

He leaned down and dropped a soft kiss onto my hair. "Nothing would please me more."

CHAPTER 22

I LAY ON a deserted beach, the sun beating down on me and the fruity cocktail on the table at my side. One of those multi-coloured ones with a little umbrella and a swizzle stick. The bikini I wore showed off smooth, tanned skin as I stretched my arms above my head and snuggled back into Linc. One of his arms snaked over my belly, his fingers splayed out, claiming me as his, not that I ever wanted to be anybody else's.

I wiggled my ass again, feeling the evidence of his happiness in the small of my back. A lot of evidence. I sighed, wondering if it was too early to head inside or whether we should stay and enjoy the sun for a few minutes longer. "Mmm, Linc."

"Morning, sweetheart. It's baking in here. Do you always leave the heating on so high?"

My eyes popped open, and I lamented my disappearing dream. I wanted to reach into my mind and pluck it back, to turn it into a reality. Okay, so some parts of it were already real, if what I could feel between my butt cheeks was anything to go by. I moved an inch. Yes, it was real all right.

"I like things hot in here."

Wrong thing to say. Or the right thing, depending on how you looked at it. I squealed as Linc flipped me over and lowered his lips onto mine.

"Lucky for you, I know how to do hot."

And Hisashi knew how to do bucket of cold water. My shriek must have woken him because his cries came through on the baby monitor seconds later. Although Sofia had one as well, I should be the one to comfort my son.

"I need to go to him."

"I know." He gave my ass one final squeeze as I rolled out of bed. At least I didn't have to bother putting a robe on, seeing as I'd fallen asleep fully clothed.

The animal mobile Bradley brought last time he came soon quieted Hisashi, although it took me almost a minute to convince him to let go of the glittery pink unicorn. By the time I did that, then changed and dressed him, Linc and Sofia were already at the breakfast bar.

"I'm making eggs," Sofia announced. "Do you want yours fried or scrambled?"

"Scrambled, please. I'll do the toast." We'd got the teamwork thing sorted.

"Guess that leaves me on juice." Linc got up and walked to the fridge.

"What time are you working today?"

"Ten 'til seven. Which means if Jansen gives you shit today, I'll kick him down the stairs."

"Has he been causing problems again?" Sofia asked.

Over breakfast, I told her about the events of the previous evening, leaving out the details of Linc's panic attack.

"That little bastard!" She addressed Linc. "Stairs are too good for him. Drop him down the elevator shaft."

"Stairs are easier."

She smiled sweetly. "I'm sure you could make it look like an accident."

"No, no accidents. We've got another recital next week, and I need to get a good grade," I said. "You might have a late start, but I've got the joys of a piano lesson at nine, so I need to go. Are you staying here for a while?"

He took a sip of orange juice. "If you don't mind?"

I leaned over and pecked him on the cheek, too self-conscious to do anything more in front of Sofia. "Of course I don't. I'll see you this evening."

Except by evening my cold had got worse, and the best I could manage was a few mouthfuls of pizza at Linc's apartment before he made me call my driver to take me home again.

By Thursday, I felt no better, but Jansen's empty seat in the afternoon music theory class filled me with hope.

"Where is he?" I hissed at Jude, keeping an eye out for Dr. Birch. She was a tiny old lady of at least seventy years old, but there was nothing wrong with her hearing. Even a whisper wouldn't go unnoticed.

Jude waved his phone. "He texted. Apparently he's caught your cold."

"Bet that's my fault as well. Does that mean he's not coming to practice?"

"He is, and I quote, practically unable to move."

I wanted to grab whoever passed their germs to me and kiss them. Hurrah! "That's the best news I've had all semester."

Jude grinned back at me. "Thought you'd be happy."

"Shhh, everyone." Dr. Birch marched to the front of the class, her cane tapping out a staccato rhythm on the wooden floor. "We'll start with the compositions you should all have completed for today."

"Does this mean we get to open a bottle of champagne?" Sofia asked, after I'd given her the joyous news about Jansen.

"Definitely. If I'd known a cold would keep him down, I'd have hung around in the doctor's office ages ago, waiting for someone to sneeze on me."

"Cold? Man flu, more like. And why stop there? I'm sure we could do something with food poisoning. Salmonella maybe? Or botulism? Campylobacter's always a good one."

I giggled as I popped the cork on one of the bottles of bubbly Bradley left in the fridge. "Sofia! I want to slow him down a bit, not kill him."

"How about norovirus?"

"What if he threw up on his violin?"

"He'd have to clean it, wouldn't he?"

We hooted with laughter as we clinked glasses, a toast to the joy a runny nose could bring.

"What's dinner?" I asked. "Is that something in the oven? My sense of smell is shot to pieces."

"Pork chops stuffed with sundried tomatoes and spinach. I've made mint choc chip ice cream for afterwards from the recipe Bradley sent."

"How do you get the time to do all that?"

She shrugged. "It's not that difficult, really, and I've always loved to experiment in the kitchen."

"I don't know what I'd do without you."

I missed Linc, but Sofia's company was a good substitute, as was the bottle of red we cracked open to go with the main course. Although strangely, it turned out she hated ice cream. Like, really hated it. She shuddered as she set my bowl on the table.

"You shouldn't have made it just for me."

"Don't worry about it. I've got waffles." She dumped a generous dollop of cream in her own dish.

"We can try something different next time. How about brownies?"

"Brownies work."

Although I could think of something far more delicious than ice cream, waffles or brownies. I sent Linc a few messages through the evening, hoping he hadn't got my cold as well, but he reported he'd gone to the gym and felt fine. The virtual kisses he sent me right before I went to sleep helped me to feel better as well.

Chapter 23

FRIDAY BROUGHT THE news that Jansen was still ill, "struggling with every breath he took," according to Jude when he plopped down beside me in the literature seminar and handed me a latte and a cookie.

"Figured we should celebrate," he said.

Too right. As well as the weekend coming up, I had my Friday night date with Linc to look forward to, and tonight he'd promised not to try cooking. Sofia said he'd asked her how to make macaroni and cheese yesterday, but he'd glazed over when she mentioned a roux.

And Sofia also promised to take Hisashi to the park in the morning, complete with a shadow from Blackwood, which meant if I wanted to stay with Linc tonight, I could. Although we'd slept in the same bed once, the thought of planning such a move and possibly doing more than sleeping terrified the logical part of me. On the other hand, my libido believed it was a brilliant idea, and I couldn't get her to shut up about it.

I compromised with myself and decided to play it by ear. Which was also what I needed to do in my final music class of the day, and without Jansen glaring at me I was note perfect.

"You look happy, ma'am," my driver said, as I slid into the car at the end of the day.

"I think I am. I finally am."

The day only got better when Linc ordered our favourite Chinese and came up with a DVD that wasn't a cartoon, porn or Star Wars. To be fair, I didn't watch much of *The Notebook* either, but it was the thought that counted.

The movie was almost at an end when it happened. I was curled up next to Linc on the sofa, my lips swollen from his kisses, drunk not just on the two glasses of wine I'd quaffed but the man beside me as well. Then his hand crept under my shirt and I froze, the fire in my veins turning to ice in an instant. Strength I didn't know I possessed surged through my muscles as I pushed him away.

"Get off! Please."

Eyes wide, he sprang back. "Sweetheart, what did I do?"

"You touched my stomach."

He fell to his knees in front of me. "Shit, I thought you were as into this as I was. I thought... I'm sorry. I... Fuck, don't cry."

I hadn't even realised I was, but when I reached up my cheeks were wet. "It's not your fault. It's me. All me. I can't stand the idea of anybody seeing my body, or touching it, and I don't know if I'll ever get over it."

"What happened? Why do you think like that?"

I shook my head, biting my lip to stop the sobs from escaping. "I can't... I just can't."

"Shhh. It doesn't matter what you look like. You'll always be beautiful to me."

"I'm not, not under my clothes. My body doesn't match the rest of me." The tears fell harder, and I cursed myself. How to turn off a man in one easy lesson. The only miracle was that he hadn't run out of the door. "Why are you still here?"

"Because I love you."

"What?" I paused mid-sniffle and stared at him.

"I love you. You're the sweetest, most amazing woman I've ever met, and whatever you're hiding underneath your sweater won't change that."

He loved me? The idea was insane. Only Hisashi's father had ever told me that, but our relationship was different. He knew what I'd been through because he'd lived it too. How could a man like Linc love someone as damaged as me? How had I let things get this far?

He deserved someone perfect, who could offer him the world, and that person wasn't me. I needed to make him understand that.

"You really think my body won't change how you feel? Dogs ripped apart the flesh on my legs, and I had to sew the wounds closed myself with a needle and thread I borrowed from the housekeeper. My body looks like Picasso did an autopsy on it, and I have another man's initials carved into my stomach. Reckon you can live with that?"

Gulping in air, I ripped at the hem of my top and dragged it upwards. Linc tried to stop me but I batted his hands away. The sound of fabric ripping tore through the air, but I didn't let go until I stood half naked in front of him. I couldn't bring myself to look down, but I knew from the horror in his eyes he saw what I refused to see.

The abstract mess of lines, arrows and misshapen flowers cut into me by a madman who fucked me when he got high. In the middle of it all, the raised scars of his initials marred my stomach, white now, faded from the angry red they used to be but hideous nonetheless. Cesar Puga. The other men called him El Perro, but to do so was an insult to canines.

When I first arrived in Virginia, I caught a glimpse of myself in the mirror one morning, and in a fit of rage I took a pair of scissors to myself and changed the P into an R. CR, the initials of Hisashi's father. I thought I'd feel better afterwards, but as the blood ran down my legs I leaned over and retched. Then I hurled the scissors at the mirror, and when they bounced off, I threw a statue of a dog that sat on the mantelpiece. Fitting. The mirror shattered but even that didn't help. Nothing did. I was ugly to my core and always would be.

Except Linc was still, there, staring at me. I tried to cover myself with my hands, but he clasped them in his own and gently pulled them away, and this time I didn't have the energy to stop him.

"You'll always be beautiful to me," he whispered in a repeat of his earlier words then curled his arm around me.

Before I could process what happened he dipped his head and swiped his tongue across each of my nipples in turn, and they hardened involuntarily.

Then he stood back and pulled off his own shirt, and it was my turn to gasp. The pecs I'd run my hands over through his shirt so many times stood firm, and his abs glistened with sweat, smooth and hard. But while his left side could have graced a calendar, his right was a mass of mangled flesh, scar tissue that rivalled my own but without the attempt at order.

My eyes widened as they met his.

"Never judge a book by its cover, Akari. It's a lesson

I know very well."

"Afghanistan?"

"I lost part of my liver, and they didn't think I'd survive the night."

I took a hesitant step forward, waiting to see what he'd do. When he didn't move, I took another until there was only an inch of air between us. When I tilted my head back to look into his eyes, I expected to see pity, but what I saw was love.

"The outside doesn't matter, sweetheart. We're all just a bunch of atoms. Carbon, hydrogen, nitrogen. The important part is our souls, and nobody can change those unless we let them."

"You're my oxygen. I can't breathe without you."

"You don't have to."

That did it. I pressed against him, feeling his cock harden against my stomach as I stood on tiptoes to claim his lips. Need overcame me and I clawed at him while he fumbled first with my zipper then with his belt. He sprang free and I stroked his length, thinking only of having him inside me.

"I promised myself we'd take this slow," he said.

"Later. We can do slow later."

"In that case, hang on. I draw the line at fucking you for the first time over a sofa."

He picked me up and carried me to the bedroom, flipping open his wallet as we went. By the time he laid me on the bed I'd snatched the condom out of his hands, impatient to do the honours. The dim glow from the lamp on the nightstand cast long shadows as I straddled him, but for once I didn't care about staying in darkness. He'd seen me, all of me, and he still loved me. That more than anything made me burn from the inside out.

As soon as he was sheathed, I lowered myself onto him, relishing the fullness. He shifted his hips, hitting exactly the right spot, and I let out a whimper. I'd loved and lost once, and the part of me that still hid in darkness, the part that thought I'd never find another man to share my heart, crept out into the light. With every move, every whisper from Linc, a little more brightness shone into my soul. And soon he had me wound up so tight I almost exploded. When he reached out a finger to stroke my most sensitive part that pleasure turned into a scream. Now, those were the kind of fireworks I liked.

"Mind the neighbours, sweetheart. These walls are thin."

Oops.

He tipped me forward, muffling my next cry with his mouth. My tongue tangled with his as I moved on top, taking his hardness until I shattered around him.

When I went limp, he rolled us so he was on top, pumping into me until he too went over the edge. I clung to him as he peppered my face with soft kisses, all the while murmuring my name.

"I love you too," I whispered.

"You just made me the happiest man alive."

He kept me awake for most of the night, and like he promised, he gave it to me slow. As well as fast, creative, and in the shower. By the time the sun rose, neither of us could move.

"You know anywhere that delivers breakfast?" I mumbled into his chest.

"I can make you something."

"Is that a good idea?"

"I can go out and buy you something."

"Better." I kissed him again, hungry for more than just food. "But maybe in a little while?"

He fed me chocolate muffins in bed, rich and decadent, and then I got my first taste of him. My new favourite food, and I never intended to share it.

"What do you want to do this afternoon?" he asked, pushing my hair off my face.

The room smelled like chocolate, sweat and sex, and I inhaled deeply, committing every nuance to memory.

"I need to get home for Hisashi. It's not fair to keep asking Sofia to look after him."

"She doesn't mind. She said she loves to spend time with him, but I do too, so why don't we take him out somewhere?"

"You'd do that with us?"

"I'd do anything with you. How about the zoo? I know he's only little, but he could still watch the animals."

Ah, the zoo. We'd only been once before, with Bradley, to the Metro Richmond Zoo in Virginia. At two months old, Hisashi hadn't understood a whole lot, but I'd adored Kumbali, the cheetah, and his companion Kago, a yellow Labrador. It served as another reminder that friendship could be found in the most unlikely of places. And the lady who ran the gift shop adored Bradley, seeing as he'd bought half of it.

So yes, I loved the idea of a trip to the zoo, and with Linc and my son, it would be even more special.

"We'll need to take my car." And I'd need to properly introduce Linc to my driver, which meant that Emmy would find out how serious things were between us.

Up until now I'd tried to keep her out of the loop, as I didn't want her meddling in Linc's life as well as mine. I knew what would follow—background checks, an interrogation and a constant stream of awkward questions about my safety. I'd be back in the spotlight. Both of us would. I'd been enjoying my relative freedom without a team of bodyguards watching my every move, and I hated the thought of giving that up now.

But the other option was to take a cab, and I preferred Hisashi to sit in a proper car seat. If I wanted to have a life with Linc, I guessed I'd have to accept Emmy would find out about it.

Boy, things were about to get difficult. But with Linc by my side, difficult didn't mean impossible. We'd get through it.

His smile broke through my worries. "Let's take a shower and get dressed then pick him up. We can grab a late lunch while we're out. How does that suit you?"

"Perfect."

CHAPTER 24

ON SATURDAY NIGHT we had to keep the noise down with Sofia sleeping just along the corridor, but Linc agreed it was best he stayed at my place so we could be up early for Hisashi on Sunday morning. My son never met his real father, and whenever I watched him with Linc, I secretly started to hope he might be interested in the job.

The biggest issue I saw looming was how to overcome the school's no fraternisation policy. After spending all Sunday with Linc, having to leave him on Monday morning and pretend for the rest of the day that I didn't know him hurt. I turned it over in my head as we went over our ensemble pieces in class, but nothing could dampen my good mood. I'd always struggled with the upbeat nature of that particular Beethoven score, but my happiness transferred to the keys and I played it like a dream. When I played the closing bars, I even got a smile out of Dr. Vasilyevich, and for once Jansen didn't come up with a snide remark.

I kept an eye out for Linc as I ate lunch, but he was keeping a low profile. What could we do about our little problem? I thought of leaving Holborn, but apart from my issues with Jansen I'd grown to love the lessons, and I'd learned so much since I started. The other option would be for Linc to leave, but I didn't even know how to broach that subject with him. Of course, with the amount of money in my bank account there was no need for him to work but would he go for that idea? In Japan the idea of a woman supporting a man was unusual, but here in America I'd heard it was more acceptable.

Maybe I could ask Sofia? Or even call Emmy? To my surprise, I'd only had one message from her since last week, a rather bland "Hope everything's going well" and a query as to whether I'd be joining them in Virginia for Christmas. I'd held off on replying until I discussed it with Linc. I'd prefer to spend the holiday with him, and I didn't know what his plans were.

Except I wanted to speak to him in person, and he needed to wax the floor in the auditorium this evening, an extra job that meant he wouldn't finish until late.

"Damn boss," he'd said early this morning when he got the message with the request. "At least it doesn't need to be done often."

With practice tomorrow, that meant I wouldn't see him until Wednesday, and I didn't want to discuss something as important as Christmas by text. But he sent me a message in the afternoon reminding me to smile, so smile I did.

"What are you grinning about?" Jansen asked me on Tuesday evening.

"Nothing."

"Well, it certainly isn't your playing. You're going too fast."

"It's supposed to be allegro."

"Yes, allegro. Not presto."

Sofia's salmonella idea sounded more attractive by the second. By the end of two hours with Il Duce, I wasn't grinning any more.

"Good day?" Clint asked as I slumped in the seat.

"Could have been better."

"There's always tomorrow, ma'am."

But tomorrow was hours away. I still had to get through the rest of tonight first. I glanced at my watch. Eight thirty. What if...?

"Take a right here."

"Pardon, ma'am?"

"Take a right."

"Where are we going?"

"I'm going to visit Linc. You know, the guy who went with us to the zoo on Saturday?"

"Do you think that's wise, ma'am? It's late, and you haven't made an appointment."

"No, it'll be fine." Clint just couldn't help being polite, could he? Calling me ma'am, suggesting an appointment to see my own boyfriend. If only more men showed that kind of respect. "It's left at the stop sign."

Linc had sent me a text as I left Holborn to say he'd come back from the gym, and I kept my fingers crossed he hadn't gone out again. And also that he wasn't watching one of those awful porn DVDs. No, I needed to put those out of my mind. Linc told me they weren't his, and I believed him. But I couldn't help looking forward to a different sort of adult entertainment. Maybe I should have bought some prettier underwear?

"Er, do you want me to wait, ma'am?"

"Maybe just for a few minutes, until I've checked he's there."

Heart skipping in time to my footsteps, I hurried up the stairs, pausing for a brief second before I rapped my knuckles on Linc's door. I'd missed his smile so much. And his...

"Who are you?" The man standing in front of me definitely wasn't Linc. I checked to make sure I had the right door, and I absolutely did. Door 102, the same as always.

"I could ask the same question, lady."

"Where's Linc?"

He shrugged. "How should I know? I haven't seen him for days. Have you tried his house?"

Hang on, his what? I stared dumbly as I tried to form words. "I-I-I thought this was his house?"

"Oh, you mean he brought you here?"

"Yes."

"He borrows the place from time to time, like a swap. Said something about it being an undercover job. Doesn't bother me. At least I get to use his pool."

Undercover job? Pool? Linc had a pool? Had he lied to me? Confusion swirled inside me as I willed myself to keep calm. No, I must have misunderstood what this other man was saying.

"Would you be able to give me directions to his house? Please?"

"Sure. Hang on." He came back half a minute later with a grubby napkin and a ballpoint pen and proceeded to draw me a lopsided map. "So it's left at the end of the road, then right, carry on about a half mile then take a left into Redwood Gardens. Number 8. You can't miss it—fucking massive, it is."

Linc was living in a big house? Not on his janitor's salary, surely? Unless it was a house-share. Yes, that must be it. Obviously he wouldn't have wanted to take me home if he was living with a group of others—that would have been more than a little awkward. But why didn't he just tell me the truth?

"Thank you." I tried to un-clench my teeth. "You've been very helpful."

"No problem. Say, when you see him would you ask him what he's done with my DVD collection? Half of it's missing."

CHAPTER 25

"ARE YOU SURE this is a good idea, ma'am?"

"Please, just drive."

He gave me a worried glance but started the engine, carefully putting on the turn signal before pulling smoothly away.

"Would you mind going a little bit faster?"

Clint remained silent, but the car did speed up infinitesimally. Inwardly, I cursed his determination to stick to the speed limit. I needed to see Linc, and I needed to do it right away.

As Clint braked at a stop light, a hideous thought popped into my mind. I was an undercover job? What if that was an under-the-covers job? Linc said he was divorced, but what if he'd lied about that too?

Back in Colombia, the two main men who held me captive cheated all the time. Over the years, I'd watched a series of women parade through their beds, each leaving more broken than the last. I never wanted to be like them.

As buildings flew past outside the windows, the streets got tidier and the houses bigger, and my confusion gave way to fear and anger. Was Linc still with his wife? Had I unwittingly become his mistress? When I screamed his name in bed at night, what was he thinking? Was he trying to remember mine?

"This is Redwood Gardens, ma'am."

Well, one thing was for sure—Linc didn't afford a home here on his income from Holborn. Number eight loomed in front of me, streetlights illuminating the manicured front lawn and the Ford Mustang parked in the driveway next to Linc's Ducati. A pickup truck stood to the side under a tree. All his? A house share? Or his and hers?

"Should I wait again?"

"Yes. Don't you dare leave."

I slammed the car door and marched up the driveway, trying to think of something smart to say but coming up empty. A wrought iron knocker in the shape of a lion graced the solid wood door, and I smacked it down as hard as I could.

Who would come? Linc? Another stranger? Or a woman?

I soon got my answer. The door swung open and Linc stood there in a robe, hair slicked back like he'd just got out the shower.

His eyes widened in recognition. "Sweetheart? What are you doing here?"

"Don't 'sweetheart' me. You lied."

"Not lied, exactly. I left a few things out."

Hearing him admit to his deceit broke something inside me, and I slapped him before I realised what I was doing.

"Like what? What didn't you tell me?"

He caught my wrist, eyes fixed on mine.

"Get off me!" Too many times men had held me down. When I tried to bring my knee up between his legs, he sidestepped faster than I'd ever seen him move and pinned me against his front, facing away.

"Let me go!"

"Only if you promise not to try that again."

His grip loosened but I stayed silent. I wasn't promising anything.

"Akari?"

"Sod off." Listen to me—I'd turned into Emmy.

"I can explain."

"What, about your undercover job? Well, it worked out, didn't it? You got me under your covers, right where you wanted me. How many others, Linc? How many?"

"How many what?"

"Women! How many women?"

"None. What the hell are you talking about? It was only you."

"What about your wife? Or whoever else lives here with you?"

"I live alone."

"Then why all the secrecy? Why not just tell me the truth, whatever it is?"

"Fine. The truth is Blackwood. I work for Blackwood, okay? I didn't tell you because I was ordered not to." His voice dropped. "I got assigned to look after you."

I went limp as the news sank in then stiffened again. "Who by? Emmy?"

"Who else?"

"I'll kill her."

He let me go and took a step back. "Good luck with that one."

"Why? Why did she do this?"

"Because when you went to Holborn you said you didn't want a team of bodyguards, and she wasn't about to let you out alone."

"So she...what? Told you to get into my panties?"

"No! My brief was to hang around at Holborn and make sure you stayed safe while you were on campus." He sat down heavily on the front step and hung his head. "I didn't think for a minute that I'd fall in love with you, but it happened."

"You lied to me from the start. On all those pretend dates..."

"They were real."

"Whatever. I spent weeks digging up the courage to tell you about my past, and all the time you knew. Didn't you?"

He didn't speak.

"Didn't you?"

"I didn't know about the scars, I swear. But I knew most of the rest."

My legs buckled underneath me and Linc leapt up, catching me before I hit the ground. He tried to carry me inside, but I grabbed the door jamb and hung on.

"I'm not going in there. I don't want to."

"All right, all right. Easy. I'll put you down." He lowered me to my feet, and I took his place on the step. After a few seconds he knelt in front of me and tried to take my hand, but I snatched it away and squashed it in my lap.

"I can't believe Emmy did this," I said. "All I wanted was a bit of freedom."

"She didn't know how far things had gone, not until the weekend. Trust me, she's furious as well."

Trust him? Yeah, right. "The driver told her about our trip to the zoo?"

"She spent most of yesterday evening chewing my

ass off about it. Her final words were 'if you hurt her, I'll make the ninth circle of hell look like a vacation.'"

"She won't really, will she?"

"Probably. Sleeping with the principal's a pretty big no-no for bodyguards." He sighed and leaned back on his heels. "Doesn't matter anyway. Anywhere's going to be hell if I'm not with you." When he looked up, there was a spark of hope in his eyes, but I soon extinguished it.

"Better get used to the heat then. All that stuff in Afghanistan, how much of that was true?"

"All of it."

"And the PTSD?"

"That's real as well. I first met Emmy back in my army days, and when I got discharged she gave me a job that wasn't going to have me flipping out every other day. I owe her a lot."

Didn't we all? I wanted to believe him, but with my world turned on its head I struggled to sort the lies from the truth. "I need to think about all this. At the moment I don't know if I ever want to see you again." He tried to take my hand once more, but I batted him away. "Stop it."

"Please don't write us off, sweetheart. I'll never lie to you again, I promise. I can quit my job, well, jobs, and it'll be just the two of us."

"You'd do that?"

"Polishing floors is the most boring thing I've ever done in my life."

"I meant Blackwood."

"Yes. I love working there, Emmy's demands aside, but for you I'd walk away."

Okay, that was big, but still... We'd got off to a

shaky start. "I've got to think this through. I'm supposed to have another recital this week, and right now I can't even remember what an octave is."

"Can't help you out there, but take the time you need. Just promise me you won't make any hasty decisions."

"I need to go now."

"I love you, sweetheart."

"Goodbye, Linc."

I fought back tears as I climbed into the car. Oh, I'd cry all right, but later. I had a phone call to make first.

"Where would you like to go, ma'am?"

"Don't 'ma'am' me. You knew what was going on as well."

"Shall I take you home?"

"Yes."

I punched Emmy's number into my phone, and it only rang once before Emmy picked up.

"Akari. I've been expecting a call."

"Why? Just tell me why?"

"Why do you think? You're almost thirty, but you've never spent any time in the real world. You wanted freedom, and we wanted to make sure you were safe and nobody took advantage of you. Come on, you have to admit, Linc was a good compromise."

"It doesn't feel like it from where I'm sitting."

"I suppose the execution of some parts of the plan could have gone a little better."

"Will you stop doing that?"

"Doing what?"

"Talking about me like I'm a name on a page. I'm a living, breathing person."

She took a deep breath, and I imagined her pacing

the room as she spoke. I'd noticed she had a habit of doing that. Her husband would block her way sometimes and point at a chair, but mostly she'd glare, step around him and carry on.

"If we had to start from the top again, we'd do things differently. It's been a learning curve for me, too. This whole love thing is confusing as hell."

"But does he love me? I have no idea now."

"He loves you enough that when I told him to back off last night he told me to go fuck myself. A physical impossibility, but luckily I have someone to take care of that for me."

Ah yes, her husband. The only other man in the world whose arms I felt safe in, even if he did scare the hell out of me at the same time.

And Linc? I didn't fear him, but right now I was so angry with him, Emmy, and the whole situation I felt I'd self-combust. "So now what? You've screwed with my heart, I fell in love with a stranger, and now I'm supposed to carry on with life? How?"

"That's a question only you can answer. Linc's gonna stick around for a while if you want him."

"I need space. Space to think."

"I'll make sure you get that."

I hung up the phone and threw it at the privacy screen in front of me. The glass cracked, but Linc's face still glowed back at me through the shards and I burst into tears. I'd been through agony in my life, but the pain of a broken heart scored through me like no other.

CHAPTER 26

"AKARI? WHAT'S HAPPENED?"

Sofia took one look at me when I walked in the door before she rushed over, worry etched across her features.

"Everything. Linc lied. Everyone lied."

"Huh? Linc lied? What about?"

I fell back on the sofa and blubbed the whole story out. The way the man I'd fallen in love with only gave me a second glance in the first place because Emmy paid him to. How I didn't know which of his feelings were real. The awful way I found out the truth this evening.

"All these little things keep falling into place. Like him not knowing his way round that apartment, and always being happy to take his bike, even if it was raining. He couldn't admit he had his own expensive cars on a janitor's salary, and he must have known if we took mine, the driver would report everything he saw back to Emmy."

I bet even when we drove to his real house, Clint tried to warn him. Too bad he'd been in the shower. Otherwise what new story would he have come up with?

"Men suck. You know what doesn't suck?"

"What?"

"Wine. And chocolate cookies. You hold still and I'll get both."

This was why I'd heard women say a good girlfriend was worth two of a man any day. Sofia knew exactly what to say and she didn't pry, just kept my glass topped up and listened to the ramblings that spilled from my mouth.

"Sho what should I dooo?" I slurred an hour later, staring into my grape juice as if it held the answers to all my problems.

"Difficult to say. For what it's worth, I think he really does love you. After you went to school the other morning and we ate breakfast together, he wouldn't stop talking about you. Kept asking me the sort of things you liked, what you didn't like. I think he planned to take you to the opera next weekend. He asked if I'd mind looking after Hisashi."

"Linc likes opera? He never told me that."

"I'm quite sure he doesn't, which is the whole point. He was going to go because you like it."

"Oh. This relationship thing's complicated." Confusing, just as Emmy said. My head swam with unanswered questions and half-thoughts. Or maybe that was the wine.

"Love is never easy," Sofia said softly. "But if you find the right person, I'm sure it's worth putting the effort in."

Was Linc worth the effort? I needed to have a serious think about the answer to that question.

"Are you okay in there?"

Sofia's voice floated through my door in the morning, permeating my brain with the subtlety of Thor and his hammer.

"Head. Hurts."

"Give me a sec. I'll bring aspirin."

A few seconds later, she came in, balancing Hisashi in one arm with a glass of water and packet of pills in the other. She put Hisashi down next to me and he crawled into my lap, waving a toy giraffe at me and chattering excitedly.

"It's too early," I groaned, reaching for the water. I swallowed down the pills Sofia popped into my hand and sipped. My throat felt like someone took a nail file to it.

"It's almost eleven."

I sat up straight. "Shit, shit! I'm late for school."

"No you're not. I already found the number and called in sick for you."

"But I have a recital on Friday. I need to practice."

"You've got a piano here, and you can play it later if you feel up to it. Right now, you're staying in bed." She smiled. "I'll lock you in this room if I have to."

I laid my head back on the pillow and groaned. She was right. No way could I sit through class feeling like this. Every time I moved someone took an ice pick to the back of my eyeballs.

A knock at the door sounded, and we looked at each other.

"Are you expecting anyone?" Sofia asked.

"No."

She got to her feet. "I'll go see who it is."

Voices came from the hallway, and despite the hushed tones I recognised one of them as Linc's. I prayed Sofia wouldn't let him in. Not only did I have no clue what to say to him yet, my mouth tasted like tar and my hair was sticking out all over the place.

"Mama's a mess," I muttered to Hisashi, laying my forehead against his.

He pinched my nose then giggled.

The voices stopped, and a door slammed. A few seconds later Sofia appeared in my doorway alone, her face clouded.

"I told him today wasn't a good day."

"I'm not sure I'll ever have a good day again."

She sat down on the edge of the bed and patted my hand. "Of course you will. It'll just take a bit of time for things to get sorted out. You'll see."

"Do you think he'll come back?"

"He seems kind of persistent."

Another unwelcome caller followed shortly after, this one by phone. Emmy. I'd have hung up on her, but if I did that I bet she'd be on the next plane from Virginia. She had a private jet and knew how to use it.

"How are you feeling today?"

"I have a headache."

"Do you want me to get someone to bring pills?"

"Sofia's here. She's looking after me. At least someone cares."

"Ouch. So you're still at home?"

"I didn't wake up until half an hour ago." And sincerely wished I hadn't.

"Are you going to school tomorrow? I'll organise someone to come with you if you are."

"Who this time? Are you going to send in someone disguised as a student?"

"Tricky. That was actually my original plan, but do

you know how hard it is to find someone who can shoot straight and play the piano? The janitor thing was a last minute solution. Linc can play about four chords on the guitar, and he only sings when he's been drinking."

Great, she knew my so-called boyfriend better than I did. "I spent weeks with the man, and now I've got no idea who he is."

"And you told him everything about you, I suppose?"

"He already knew."

"That's not the point."

Was she right? True, Linc had been more open with me about his time in Afghanistan than I had about my life in Colombia, but I didn't have a secret life as a covert agent I'd conveniently forgotten to mention. That was a fairly big sticking point.

"So is there anybody else undercover at school that I should know about?" I didn't expect her to give me a straight answer, but I figured I might as well ask.

"No. I'll send three bodyguards with you tomorrow. When you're not in your building, you need protection."

"No way. I just want to fit in. Is that too much to ask?"

"They can wait in the corridor."

"Car park."

"Lobby."

"Fine." That was as close as anyone ever got to a compromise with Emmy. "At least they can trip Jansen up if he behaves like an asshole."

"You want me to arrange that?"

Oh shit, did I say that last bit out loud? "Forget it. He's just an irritation I could do without."

"I've been made aware. I'm dealing with the problem, but it might take a couple of weeks. He's not quite as stupid as Brigitte."

Did she mean with the "art" film? "So that was you? You got her expelled?"

"Of course. Linc alerted me to her bitchiness straight away. Believe it or not, I'm only trying to help."

I knew deep down that was the truth. Emmy had done a lot for me, including saving my life, and Hisashi's too. She went above and beyond in her quest to look after her friends and family. But sometimes I couldn't help wishing she'd stop.

CHAPTER 27

"HE'S ON THE phone. Do you want to talk to him?" Sofia stuck her head through the door, waving my mobile.

"No. I still don't know what to say."

Day two after Linc's secret came out, and I felt every bit as bad as I did the day before. The only people I wanted to see were Sofia and Hisashi, and although it was only eleven o'clock I'd already got through a glass of wine, half a cheesecake and three quarters of a box of chocolates.

"No problem. I'll put him off."

Bradley rang with...condolences? Commiserations? Something like that. He offered to fly out, but I told him to stay in Virginia. No point in messing up his life as well. He told me to expect a package soon, and I dreaded to think what would be in it. Maybe half a florist store and a vat of chocolate?

For the rest of the morning and the start of the afternoon, I watched mindless talk shows, which helped a little. Some of the guests were truly scary. My life may be in the toilet, but at least my boyfriend hadn't cheated on me with my half-sister's parrot. Sofia roused me from my stupor at three, clutching the phone in her hand again.

"Jude's asking for you. Should I tell him you're not

available?"

"No, it's okay. I'll speak to him."

I'd given him my number at the start of the semester, but until now he'd never called me. What did he want?

"Hello?"

"Hitler's on the warpath."

"You mean Jansen?"

"Who else? He got so narked earlier when he found out you weren't at school he threw his textbook through the window."

"Why was it open? It's freezing outside."

"No, I mean through the window. Glass went everywhere."

"He's crazy."

"Tell me something new. So are you coming in for practice?"

"I can't."

"You know the recital's tomorrow, right?"

Playing in front of an audience was the last thing I felt like doing, but I needed the grade. Plus, I didn't want to let the others down, even if Jansen was an idiot. "I'll be there. I'll practice at home tonight."

"You'd better be. Jansen's going to blow if you're not."

"I'll be there," I repeated.

For a moment I contemplated heading straight for the airport and catching the next flight to Japan. I could be home by the time I was due at the recital. But I quickly dismissed that idea. It may help short term, but I'd have to deal with my family's disappointment, and the mess in Boston would get more difficult to sort out the longer I ran.

No, I needed to focus. Practise for the recital first then think about what to say to Linc. That was my plan.

I pulled a fluffy white robe over my pyjamas and shuffled through to the lounge. Sofia was sprawled next to Hisashi, pointing at pictures of animals and trying to get him to say the words.

"Cow."

"Caaaa."

"No, honey. Cow."

At least the pair of them were busy. I slid onto the stool in front of the Fazioli and began to play, but my hands were so heavy, my touch so harsh, even Hisashi hated it. He screamed long and loud, and Sofia picked him up to comfort him.

"I'm sorry. It's not going well today," I said. The jolly notes of Beethoven were at odds with my black mood, and my attempts sounded like a flock of monkeys had got loose at the keys.

"I'll take him through to the nursery. We can play in there for a while."

"Thank you. That's probably best."

The next day, a capacity crowd waited in the recital hall, more than attended either of the previous events. As I walked to the stage, hundreds of eyes followed me, almost as if they were waiting to witness my impending humiliation. In the back row, the three bodyguards who accompanied me from home sat like statues, arms folded. Did Emmy train them to do that?

I took my place at the keys and arranged my music on the stand. Usually I didn't need it, but the notes wouldn't stay in my head this time. Competing for space with Linc, there could only be one winner.

He'd messaged me this morning, a simple line that said *Good luck x*. He didn't bother telling me to smile this time. He must have known it would be an impossibility.

Dr. Vasilyevich tapped his microphone, asking for silence. "I wish to introduce our fourth ensemble of the day. Jansen van Diemen, Jude Radley and Akari Takeda."

As soon as my fingers struck the first note, I knew I'd made a mistake in coming. Why hadn't I made up an excuse and stayed in bed? Emmy would have thought of something convincing.

Where the music should have been smooth, it resonated with a jaggedness that came from my soul. Harsh and lumpy, it cut right through me, and Jansen and Jude too if their glares were anything to go by. I missed a chunk of notes in the middle, started to repeat the beginning of the fifth page, and played on when there should have been silence. I wasn't imagining the steam coming from Jansen's ears as he finished his own part with a flourish.

As soon as the lights went up, I fled the stage, running up the steps and shoving through the door to the corridor. Footsteps followed, and I prayed they belonged to the three stooges rather than Jansen. I couldn't deal with him right now. I didn't slow until I'd left the whispers in the auditorium far behind.

Where was I? I looked around, trying to get my bearings. My blind dash through hallways and down stairs had led me to Linc's palace in the basement, only now the door lay ajar. I peeped in. Empty. Not just of

Linc but all his belongings, too. Tears started afresh when I realised he'd left his job at Holborn. If I'd thought logically I'd have known he would, but that didn't make it any easier to take.

The bodyguards caught up with me and skidded to a halt a few feet away, shifting from foot to foot as they waited for me to do something.

Finally, the tallest one stepped forward. "Do you want to go home, ma'am?"

I nodded, even though my apartment no longer felt like a home. Home had been Linc, and now I was destitute, cast out on the street until I figured out a way to come back in from the cold.

CHAPTER 28

"DO YOU WANT to come to the park with us? Or maybe the aquarium?" Sofia asked.

She'd got Hisashi up and dressed already while I still lay in bed, crumbs from the packet of biscuits I'd eaten last night scratchy against my skin. The tequila bottle taunted me from the nightstand. Empty. That would explain my headache.

I groaned and tried to sit up, my muscles protesting. "It's your day off. I can take care of him."

She shot me a look that said I was being ridiculous. "Don't be silly. You've had a terrible week, and I'm not leaving you on your own." The bed dipped as she perched on the edge. "You're not just my employer; you're my friend."

Her words made my heart swell a little. True friends were difficult to come across, and while I might have lost one this week, I'd gained another. "I really appreciate that."

"Have you thought any more about the Lincoln situation?"

Only the rest of yesterday and most of the night. "A bit."

"And? I really think you should talk to him."

Apart from a couple of phone calls, which Sofia intercepted, he'd kept his distance. Yes, Emmy promised to make him stay away, but it still hurt a little that he hadn't tried to come and see me after that initial attempt. But then again, he knew Emmy, and she'd probably rigged up a minefield around the building to stop him from getting in.

"Maybe I'll call him later."

Sofia shook her head as if she didn't believe me and got up. "I'll make breakfast. Take a shower, and the food will be waiting for you when you get out."

Sometimes she could be as bossy as Emmy, but I suppose I needed that. I lifted the quilt and gave myself a delicate sniff. Okay, I definitely needed that.

An hour later, I'd eaten pancakes with maple syrup and swallowed the handful of vitamins Sofia put by my plate. I didn't quite feel human yet, but I was less dead than the zombie-Akari I'd been earlier. Sofia finished loading the dishwasher and sat on the stool opposite me, Hisashi on her lap. He wrapped his fingers around the dark brown hair she habitually wore loose, and waved his other hand at me.

"Feeling better?"

"A tiny bit," I admitted.

"Linc called again while you were in the shower."

"What did he say?"

"Just that he'll never stop loving you, and please would you talk to him. Akari, he sounded like a broken man." Even Sofia, who'd listened to my tales of everything he'd done, sounded a little sorry for him.

"What do you think I should do?"

"Hear him out, at least. If you don't like what he's

got to say, you don't have to see him again, but at least you'd be able to make that decision with more information than you've got at the moment."

"He lied to me."

"I know. But from what he said, he was stuck between his feelings for you and his job. By the time he realised he was in love with you, the charade had gone so far it was difficult for him to turn back."

"Difficult, but not impossible. He didn't even try."

"If he'd told you one day over coffee, would you have reacted differently?"

"Well, uh..." The truth was, probably not. It would have felt like he'd stabbed me through the heart no matter how he'd revealed his true identity.

"Exactly. Just give him a chance to talk to you."

She was right, wasn't she? I needed to talk to him, and I couldn't put it off forever. The pain over his absence hadn't eased in the slightest. What if it never did? "If I ask him to come over, will you stick around?"

"Absolutely."

"Could you pass the phone?"

My hand shook as I waited for him to pick up, but that only lasted for a second. His voice came down the line almost immediately. "Akari?"

"Yes."

"Sweetheart, are you okay? I've been so worried about you."

"I don't know. We need to talk."

"Anytime. Now?"

"Not on the phone. Can you come over?"

"I'm on my way."

I paced the lounge, waiting for Linc to arrive. How long would he take to get here? Half an hour? Twenty minutes if he broke all the speed limits?

I'd got dressed in a pair of black pants and an embroidered silk blouse, then decided that looked like I was trying too hard and changed into jeans and a sweater. Was the lipstick too much? I stared at my gaunt reflection in the mirror before grabbing a tissue and wiping it off. A mirror I'd refused to look in before he'd changed me. Did I really want to go back to how I was before?

"Can I do anything to help?" Sofia asked.

"Is there any more wine?"

She gave me a sharp look. "Too early. Talk first, then wine. Although you might find you don't need it."

"Maybe." Or maybe I'd need a bucket to vomit into instead. Right now, the pancakes I'd enjoyed an hour ago were making their presence known again. I looked at my watch. He'd be here any minute.

"You promise you won't leave?"

"I'll take Hisashi into the nursery, but I'm not going anywhere. Holler if you need me."

The entry phone trilled and I jabbed the button, pushing my hair out of my face with my other hand. Sofia melted away, and seconds later there was a knock at the door. Linc must have run up the stairs.

I closed my eyes and took a deep breath as I reached and pulled the door open. The next few minutes would decide my future. Would it be heaven or hell?

A hard shove to my chest sent me reeling backwards and I overbalanced, tripping over my own feet before my ass hit the floor. I shook my hair out of my eyes, trying to process what just happened.

"Get up, bitch."

"Jansen?"

He glared down at me, eyes narrowed, but I barely looked at his face. My eyes focused on the big black gun he held in his hand, the muzzle pointed right at my head. My heart pounded as I recalled Puga and his revolver, and all the others who'd threatened me in Colombia. Back then I hadn't cared if I'd died, but now I wanted to live. Wouldn't that be ironic? Surviving fifteen years of torture in the jungle only to die in an apartment in Boston. The place I was supposed to be safe.

And where was Sofia with my son? Did she hear Jansen come in?

"Do you know what grade our group got yesterday? Do you?"

I shook my head hurriedly as I struggled to my feet. Grades had been the last thing on my mind when I fled the building.

"A D, Akari. A fucking D. They said our group lacked cohesion, and we showed a clear lack of practice."

"I-I-I'm sorry."

"You will be. I don't tolerate mistakes, Akari, and you've screwed up twice now. I'll never get to play for the world's top orchestras with a transcript like the one I have at the moment, and that's all your fault."

He'd lost his damn mind. "I'll speak to the dean. I'll tell him it was me. I'll tell him you practised every day, and it was me who messed everything up."

"You think that'll do any good? He already called me in yesterday for a little chat. Said he'd received complaints about my attitude. *My* attitude? I'm not the one who keeps skipping practice for frivolous reasons."

"I'll make it up to you, I promise."

"I don't believe you. You have so much talent but you choose to waste it, day after day. I've seen you chase after that deadbeat. You've let him steal your attention when it should have been on making music. But no more. I'll make sure he can't distract you any longer."

What did he mean? The way he was waving the gun around, I had a horrible idea of his plans.

"I-I-I'm not with him. I saw sense and realised I needed to focus on the music, especially after yesterday."

His mouth set in a hard line. "I'm not sure I trust you. Women are all the same, liars and cheats. I thought it might be different in America, but time after time you've proven me wrong."

And with Linc on his way here, in a minute or two I'd look like a liar once again. I needed to get Jansen out of the apartment before Linc arrived. Visions of Linc's face danced before my eyes, first with a smile, then falling backwards with a hole in his forehead. I'd witnessed that sight too many times in Colombia. With the men who held me captive, execution was as routine as brushing their teeth in the morning.

My son, Linc, Sofia. All the people I cared about, in danger.

"I'll prove you right. Why don't we go and practice right now, you and me? We'll be note perfect at the next recital." Or dead. I tried to tamp down the feeling of panic welling up inside, all the time listening for the dreaded buzz of the entry phone.

"You understand that if you let me down again, I'll need to look for a new pianist?"

"I do. Please, give me another chance."

He motioned me towards the door with the gun and I took a hesitant step, terrified of what would happen next. Would he take me to Holborn? Would anyone see me arrive? Although there were no lessons at the weekend, students had key cards for the practice rooms, but from what I'd heard the place was like a ghost town.

At least Sofia would know I'd gone. Could she hear the conversation? I raised my voice in the hope she might.

"Are you taking me to Holborn?"

"Where else?"

I prayed for Sofia to tell Linc everything. He'd get Blackwood involved, and they'd have a better chance of getting me out of this mess than the police, of that I was confident. "The usual practice room?"

"Does it matter? Hurry up and move."

We were almost at the door when Hisashi's cry cut through the air, a seldom-heard wail that he only did when he got spectacularly upset about something. Jansen stopped.

"What's that?"

"Uh, I must have left the TV on."

Hisashi cried out again, wrenching at my heart. Please, Sofia, keep him quiet!

"No, that's not a TV. You have a baby here?"

"Leave him alone!" Not caring about the gun, I ran

at him, my only thought to stop him from getting to my son. I'd almost got within striking distance when he backhanded me, sending me reeling back against the coffee table. Stars twinkled and pain shot through my neck as I caught my head on the corner, and when I tried to get up again my limbs wouldn't work. All I could do was watch helplessly as Jansen strode towards the nursery.

He kicked the door open and marched inside. The door hung open, and shadows danced on the wall as muffled thumps echoed from the room. Sofia. He'd found Sofia.

Then a gunshot, loud enough to make my ears ring.

Strength I didn't know I possessed sent me to my knees and I half-crawled, half-stumbled towards the nursery. Only silence came from within, no more sounds of a struggle. Oh fuck, tell me he hadn't killed my son. Or Sofia. Or both.

I grasped the doorframe and used it to pull myself to my feet, almost too scared to look. But I had to.

"You okay?" Sofia rose from a crouch, fingers red with blood. "Don't worry, there's no pulse."

"You shot him?" A stupid question, seeing as there was a gaping hole in the back of Jansen's head.

"Yeah." She stood back and assessed him critically. "A little off-centre, though."

Huh? This wasn't the Sofia I knew. I looked at her again, expecting to see horror in her eyes, but what I saw was... nothing. They were flat, as dead as Jansen's.

Then another wave of fear struck me. "Where's Hisashi?"

She waved in the direction of the en-suite. "In the bath. Cast iron. It was the safest place for him."

A crash sounded from behind us, and seconds later a man rushed into the room. Without his beard, it took me a few moments to realise it was Linc.

"Akari, are you okay?"

Was I? I sagged back against the wall and took stock of the situation. I was alive, my son was alive, Sofia was alive. Things were far from okay, but I nodded anyway.

Then Linc focused on Sofia, who raised an eyebrow.

"What the fuck, Fia?"

She shrugged then a grin popped onto her face. "Problem solved."

I stared at both of them. "What the hell is going on?"

"Sweetheart, I can explain."

CHAPTER 29

EMMY ARRIVED TWENTY minutes later, and by then I was sitting on the sofa, knees drawn up in front of me as I cradled Hisashi on my lap. The first thing she did was peer in at the body before walking back into the lounge and embracing Sofia in a long hug.

"Nice job, honey."

"Saves us a bit of trouble, anyway."

I interrupted their little...well, obviously it was a reunion. "Would you tell me what the hell is going on? Nobody will speak to me."

Apart from Linc, but when I'd tried to slap him again he backed off to the safety of the kitchen.

Emmy sat next to me. I felt like smacking her as well, but I knew I'd never get away with it. "It's simple. You didn't want bodyguards, but there was no way we'd let you or Hisashi go unprotected. You got Linc, Hisashi got Fia."

And by "we" she meant her and her husband. I looked up as he walked into the room, although there was no need. As soon as he darkened the threshold, it felt like all the air had been sucked out of the apartment. He nodded in my direction then went through to the kitchen.

I closed my eyes and leaned back. The two people closest to me in Boston, those I thought I could trust, and they'd betrayed me. "They both lied."

"Technically Linc didn't lie. He just left stuff out. Fia, yeah, she wasn't exactly truthful."

I thought back to when I'd hired her. Her perfect CV, the background check done by Bradley. "Is she even a nanny at all?"

"No, but she held a baby once and read a couple of books." She held up a hand to stop the tirade I was about to unleash. "Don't worry. She had a team of people helping her at all times when you weren't here, and even when you were she wore an earpiece in case she got stuck. How do you think she got through the interview?"

"A team of people?" My stomach felt hollow.

Emmy counted off on her fingers. "A childcare expert, a paediatrician, a chef, a cleaner." She looked up at Sofia, standing silently next to her. "Did I miss anyone?"

"There was an intern I used for errands." She took a seat beside Emmy. "Just be thankful you didn't have to eat my cooking. My attempt at chocolate brownies was a fucking disaster."

Emmy grimaced. "I still remember the time you insisted on barbecuing that armadillo in Borneo. I'd rather have eaten the firewood."

An armadillo? "Look, Sofia's lack of cooking skills is the last thing I care about. How could you take over my life like this?"

"To keep you safe. If we hadn't been here, you'd probably be in the morgue by now. Jansen was unhinged. He covered his tracks well, but the Dutch police found the body of his previous practice partner in a lake last week. What's left of her was only identified yesterday afternoon."

I tried to maintain my cool as dizziness came over me. "He killed her?"

"Apparently she'd complained about him pushing her too hard, so it looks like he gave her a final shove. Until a fisherman found the body, everyone reckoned she'd moved home to Korea to look after her sick mother."

Breathe, just breathe. "I can't believe it."

"Neither did the dean at the Conservatorium van Amsterdam. Apparently, he thought Jansen was just a little highly strung. The dead girl and a few others complained about his attitude, but Jansen's daddy made a healthy donation to the school's building restoration project and the details got left off Jansen's transcript."

I shuddered at my narrow escape, but that still didn't excuse Emmy's behaviour entirely.

"I'm grateful you kept me safe, but why did you do it in such an underhand way?"

"You said you didn't like the suits following you round all the time. Besides, Fia's worth ten of them. And you liked Linc, admit it."

"What were you doing? Feeding each other information?"

Sofia spoke up. "I report to Emmy. Linc was a junior member of the team, and he didn't know I was here until last week when you decided to pop round with him unexpectedly. We had a little chat the next morning, and I explained the benefits of keeping his mouth shut."

"You threatened him?"

"I prefer 'persuaded.'"

I let out a thin breath. Dammit. She really was just Emmy 2.0. "So now what? I don't suppose you'll let me live my life as I want it, will you?"

Emmy's husband made a reappearance, his massive frame materialising beside me. "Sorry. You're family. We take care of family." He smiled, making my heart break all over again as I remembered the way Hisashi's father used to give me the same look. "Whether they like it or not."

If I'd found all this out yesterday, I'd have taken my son and run to the ends of the earth, but with Jansen's body still in the nursery I had to admit they'd got a point. "But this is all such a mess."

"We'll clear it up. Fia did the sensible thing and shot the bastard in the face, so it's easy enough to claim self-defence. We'll have a cleaning crew go through and clear up the blood, and I believe Bradley's already arranging for a new carpet."

He only ever considered the practicalities. Not the destruction of my sanctuary and my sanity. "I meant about the whole protection situation."

He looked at Emmy and raised an eyebrow.

"I could do with Fia back," she said. "She's still got the Ice Cream Project to work on, and this was only ever a temporary solution."

"Fine." He turned back to me. "We'll find you a new nanny, a proper one this time. And we'll bring the bodyguards back, but try to make them a bit more subtle."

I groaned. "Round the clock?"

"Yes. Three in the day, two outside at night. Or Linc in here. Your choice."

Movement outside the kitchen door caught my eye

as Linc walked into the room. Without the beard I caught sight of a strong, angular jaw that made my heart do funny things.

He smiled, a tentative quirk of his lips that let me know he was as unsure about this as I was. I had a decision to make. Should I let him back into my life again?

I slid forward and went to hand Hisashi to Sofia, an automatic gesture, but I stopped myself at the last minute when he burst into tears.

"Sorry, I had to poke him earlier to make him cry. I don't think he likes me any more."

I glared at her as Emmy's husband held his arms out instead, and Hisashi reached for him. The man may be heartless most of the time, but there was no doubt he loved my son. Hisashi snuggled into his arms as I took a step towards Linc.

"We need to talk."

"I know, sweetheart, I know."

A couple of Blackwood employees stood chatting by the sink, but when we walked into the kitchen they melted away.

I climbed onto a stool, my legs no longer willing to hold me up. Linc reached out a hand but I shook my head, and he pulled another seat up next to me. We stared at each other, neither of us sure where to start.

After a painful silence, Linc spoke. "I'm sorry. Sorry for everything I didn't tell you and for pretending to be something I wasn't. But I'm not sorry for loving you. I never will be."

"How can we move on from here? Every day I find out something else that people have lied to me about. When will it end?"

"I get the impression Emmy's been doing a bit of thinking about that. If you ask her questions now she'll probably tell the truth. I reckon you caught her by surprise with the move to Boston, then your refusal to have guards, and she was left scrambling to come up with a solution at short notice."

"You and Sofia? Anyone else?"

"Nobody undercover that I know of."

"Why you?"

He leaned his elbows on the counter and sighed. "After Afghanistan, my life went to shit. My wife left me when the panic attacks started, and the army was all I'd ever known. Then I found nobody wanted to hire a washed-up ex-soldier. I'd worked with Emmy on a couple of missions in the Middle East, and she was the one who gave me a chance when nobody else would. When she asked me if I'd do what was supposed to be a straightforward undercover job for a few months, I was happy to help out. Plus, it meant I got to spend some time in my home town."

"Have you done that kind of job a lot?"

"Normally I work for Nick Goldman, looking after celebrities. You know Nick?"

I nodded.

"Never met one of those I wanted to spend the rest of my life with. Most of them are a pain in the ass."

He wanted to spend his life with me? His delivery was matter of fact, but his words hit deep.

"And Sofia? She said you didn't know she was here?"

"Not until you mentioned her name a couple of weeks ago. Got me thinking. Figured I wouldn't put something like that past Emmy then when we met I recognised her."

"She scared the shit out of me earlier when she shot Jansen. I still can't stop shaking."

He reached out and took my hand, and this time I didn't stop him. "Fia Darke scares the crap out of me, too."

"Darke? She told me her name was Drake."

"She's Darke by name and Darke by nature."

"In what way?"

"I don't know specifics, but I've heard enough about her to realise she's not a woman whose toes you want to tread on."

"Why her? Why did Emmy send her out of all people?"

"They go way back, but no one really knows what the relationship is there. I heard Fia ran into some problems on a job recently and needed to take a break from the sharp end. Emmy probably asked her for a favour as well."

"Emmy said something about an ice cream project just now. Do you know what that is?"

"Above my pay grade." His face was open, his eyes fixed on mine. I knew he spoke the truth now, but something still bothered me.

"How did Emmy get here so fast? She never told me she was in Boston."

"We started digging into Jansen more deeply earlier in the week when things escalated." He hung his head. "I miscalculated. Until then I thought he was more of an irritation, not a serious threat."

"It's not your fault."

"I should have realised." His eyes closed, and I saw he wrongly blamed himself. "Anyway, I wasn't in the loop for all of it, but I heard Emmy flew in to help Fia deal with him."

"What do you mean 'deal with him?'" I thought back to Sofia's blank look after she shot him, and her nonchalant "problem solved." "Actually, forget it. I don't want to know."

My mouth was dry, and I got up to fetch a glass of water. Okay, so it wasn't so much out of thirst but a desire to put off the next part of the conversation. I fussed around adding ice cubes and a slice of lemon until Linc cleared his throat behind me.

Okay, no more stalling. "I guess we need to talk about the future."

"Is that a good sign? I mean, do you want us to have one?"

"Everything's such a mess in my head. I only know that every time I think of living my life without you in it everything turns grey." Although we'd had our problems, the way he treated me, with compassion and respect, outweighed a lot of the bad. And I couldn't forget the way he cared for my son. That had to count for something.

He took my hand again, this time holding it against his chest. "Same. It's like somebody turned the lights out."

"But I can't forget everything that's happened."

"I'd never expect you to."

"Could we try and start again? So I can get to know the real you?"

"Anything."

"But if you lie to me again, that's it. I can't take any more days like this one." My heart wouldn't last through another betrayal. Once, being alone scared me but it was preferable to a wounded soul.

He looked me straight in the eye. "Akari, I promise I'll never lie to you again."

I reached out for his other hand. "Then let's see what we can make of this."

EPILOGUE

"BIRD!" HISASHI POINTED through the kitchen window. "Feeeeenix."

He knew phoenix, flamingo and toucan but struggled with crow. Damn Bradley and his exotic gifts. Since last month, my son had been obsessed with My Little Pony, and I wasn't quite sure what to do about it.

Linc was little help. "Maybe we could buy him a truck. One of those electric ones."

"He's not even two."

"It's never too early to learn."

And Linc spent a lot of time teaching him things. When I went back to school he'd begun caring for Hisashi in the day, albeit with the help of a new nanny, or au pair as Emmy called her, seeing as she was from Europe. Despite Linc leaving Blackwood, we hadn't managed to escape its clutches completely, and our new assistant was the daughter of Blackwood Germany's regional head.

"She just wants to experience a different culture," Emmy had said, when she first broached the subject, and having been in that position myself I agreed to the idea.

What Emmy failed to mention was that Monique was a champion pistol shooter and spent her spare time kickboxing. I couldn't win them all.

The other reminder of Emmy's reach was the bodyguard who accompanied me whenever Linc wasn't by my side. True to her word, Emmy had toned their presence down a bit, but the newest recruit still looked stiff as he carried his violin case at his side. Goodness only knows what he kept stashed away in there. Emmy promised he'd blend in quickly—apparently he'd spent the last six months on tour with a rock band and the peace and quiet unsettled him.

Speaking of violins, our ensemble had a new member. Sabine was a timid girl, but played with a fiery passion she didn't show in other facets of her life. Best of all, she didn't exhibit any psychopathic tendencies and seemed content to practice with Jude and I twice a week.

"Are you ready to go, sweetheart?" Linc asked, appearing in the doorway with his keys in his hand. "I've put Hisashi's stuff in the car."

I couldn't wait. We'd decided to go hiking, and after days of rain the weather gods had blessed us with brilliant sunshine. I took a last look around Linc's house to make sure we hadn't forgotten anything. No, not Linc's house. *Our* house. We'd made it official last week when I handed back the keys to my old apartment. Since Jansen died there it gave off bad vibes, a constant reminder of the pain of my past. After three months I couldn't stand it any longer. I'd only lasted a month and a half before I let Linc back into my bed, and with the amount of time we spent together it seemed pointless to keep two homes.

I'd worried about what the landlord might say, not only regarding the lease but the whole dead body issue, but Emmy confessed that her husband owned the property. An emergency purchase, she called it. See what I mean? I could never escape her clutches.

A day in the hills gave us a welcome break from city life. Linc carried Hisashi while I took the bag with the picnic, and we found a picnic table in a clearing where we could eat lunch with nature. I hoped to teach Hisashi that animals didn't always come in pink, green and orange.

"You want juice or water?" I asked Linc.

"Juice, and can you pass one of those biscuit things for Hisashi?"

I reached into the bag then froze as a twig cracked behind us. Linc heard it too, and reached to the small of his back. I knew he had a gun there—Emmy insisted on it.

Over the past months, we'd become our own therapists. I talked about my past and confronting it became easier to handle. And after weeks of hesitation, Linc headed to the gun range with a buddy from Blackwood and faced the noise again. He'd shed more than a few tears that night, we both did, but the next week he went back. And the one after, and the one after that. We were both healing, slowly.

Now, I turned to look at the woods. "Do they have bears here?" I whispered.

"Nope."

"You think it's a deer?"

"Maybe. Or maybe a lesser-spotted Blackwood employee."

I groaned. "Why doesn't that surprise me?"

Emmy just couldn't help herself. With Linc's experience in the field, he was far better at picking them out than I was, and we'd grown used to it now.

"Look." He pointed to the sky above my head.

Just over the tree line, a black helicopter was visible for a second then it disappeared. "At least we'll never get lost. All we'd have to do is wave our arms and half a dozen ninjas would pop out and point us in the right direction."

"But it does mean I can't lean you back over this table and kiss you senseless. I'm not giving them a show."

"Maybe we should head home soon."

He grinned. "You can't get enough of me, can you?"

"Never."

Without any warning, he swept me off my feet and spun me around. "Right answer."

On a Sunday two months later, the doorbell interrupted breakfast, and I paused with the spoon halfway to Hisashi's mouth.

"Should I get that?" Monique asked.

She had her hands buried in a mixing bowl, making bread she said came from her grandma's special recipe. I'd peered at her ears carefully whenever she wasn't looking for the first few weeks, anxious to check for hidden communications. Thankfully she came up clean.

"I'll go. It's only Sabine. We're practising before the concert tomorrow."

It would be our first important test, so much bigger than recital, and we'd be playing one of Beethoven's pieces as a duo. I fed the spoonful to Hisashi then went to open the door, remembering to look through the peephole first. I'd learned my lesson there.

Sabine looked away, shy as ever. "I brought fresh croissants."

Croissants, a piano, a perfect son, and Linc riding up and down shirtless on the mower in the backyard. What more could a girl want?

I gave her a quick hug. With Linc's help, I was gradually getting over my fear of touching people, starting small at first. "Shall we start?"

"Sure."

We'd got through our piece three times when her phone beeped with a message. Although she played on, her eyes kept flicking to the screen.

"Oh, just look at it. Is it from him?"

She put down her bow and flicked the screen. "Yeah. Again."

Jude messaged at least twice a day. Even though he'd flown back to England to attend his cousin's wedding in rural Berkshire, he was still thinking of her. Ever since he'd asked her out on a date a few days after she joined Holborn, and she'd told him she wasn't into party animals, he'd tried to change. More cello, less karaoke. It showed in his playing and his attitude. And even though she kept turning him down, Sabine liked him too. I could tell.

"Are you going to put him out of his misery yet?"

She smiled her shy smile. "I'm considering it."

"Please say yes. If I eat any more of the chocolates he keeps bringing you, I won't fit into my clothes."

"Okay, okay. I'll—" The doorbell rang, another interruption.

"I'll get it." Linc walked through the music room, wiping his hands on a cloth, and I completely lost my place. I gave up trying to play entirely when he came back. "Look who came to visit."

"Heard you were playing in a big concert tomorrow, so we thought we'd stop by to see if you needed any moral support. How's things?" Emmy sat on the sofa and crossed her ankles, and Sofia dropped down beside her, while Sabine put her violin back on its stand and perched next to me.

Moral support? They'd probably toss anyone who didn't applaud out on the pavement. "That sounds lovely. Would you like something to drink?"

"Why not?"

Monique appeared in the doorway. "I'll make coffee."

Emmy was her usual evasive self while Sofia stayed quiet. She did take Hisashi on her lap for a few minutes, and he seemed to have forgiven her for the poking episode. I couldn't help wondering who the real Sofia was—the sweet girl who lived with me, the cold monster who shot Jansen, or the almost mute woman sitting next to Emmy. One woman, three different faces.

I didn't get to the bottom of the puzzle that day and suspected I never would. One drink later, and they got to their feet. Emmy drew a package from her handbag. "Bradley sent a gift."

"Will you thank him for me?"

"Sure. Or call him. He loves to talk to you."

I still struggled with this socialising thing although I was getting better. A new couple had moved in across the street last week, and when they came over to introduce themselves, I invited them round for a barbecue. Little steps.

"Okay, I'll call."

She leaned in for another hug followed by Sofia, who reached her arms around me awkwardly.

"See you tomorrow." Emmy stood on tiptoe and waved at Linc then walked out the door.

Wait. What? I blinked a couple of times, unsure whether my eyes were playing tricks on me. Why did Sofia just wink at Sabine?

WHAT'S NEXT?

THE BLACKWOOD ELEMENTS series will continue with Lithium - keep an eye on Elise's website for the release date!

Lithium

Every girl loves ice cream, right?

Not Sofia. She's tried all the flavours, but plain old Vanilla was her downfall.

A trip to the Cayman Islands to give her ex what he deserves is made all the more complicated by her fear of water—not easy to handle at the best of times, but he's taken up residence on a yacht.

She cooks up a special recipe for revenge, and it's a dish best served chilled. But will handsome stranger Leo add some unwanted heat into the kitchen?

If you'd like to know more about Akari's history, you can find that in the Blackwood Security series, starting with Pitch Black.

Pitch Black

Even a Diamond can be shattered...

After the owner of a security company is murdered,

his sharp-edged wife goes on the run. Forced to abandon everything she holds dear—her home, her friends, her job in special ops—she builds a new life for herself in England. As Ashlyn Hale, she meets Luke, a handsome local who makes her realise just how lonely she is.

Yet, even in the sleepy village of Lower Foxford, the dark side of life dogs Diamond's trail when the unthinkable strikes. Forced out of hiding, she races against time to save those she cares about. But is it too little, too late?

Warning
If you want sweetness and light and all things bright,
Diamond's not the girl for you.
She's got sass, she's got snark, and she's moody and dark,
As she does what a girl's got to do.

And if you'd like a free book, read on...

For an author, every review is incredibly important. Not only do they make writers feel warm and fuzzy inside, readers consider them when making their decision whether or not to buy a book.

If you enjoyed Oxygen, it would be amazing if you took a few minutes to let the rest of the world know. Even a line saying you enjoyed the book, or what your favourite part was, helps a lot.

Better still, if you write a review for this book and email Elise a link to it at <u>elise@elise-noble.com</u>, she'll send you a free copy of one of her eBooks (you pick which one).

You can also keep up with news of Blackwood and Elise's other books by visiting her website, <u>www.elise-noble.com</u>, and signing up to her newsletter.

END OF BOOK STUFF

WHY IS IT I can write a whole novel without a problem, but when it comes to the bits at the back I'm at a loss for words?

Okay, so Oxygen came about when I decided Akari needed her own story. Emmy rather overshadowed her in Forever Black, and I wanted to know more about who she was. Why a pianist? Because every day my own piano reminds me I don't have enough time to play at the moment, and I was trying to offset some of the guilt.

I've got a few more Elements books planned too—stories I want to tell but which don't fit in the main Blackwood series for whatever reason—too much romance, not enough romance, or, in case of Rhodium, too damn filthy (Mum, please don't read that one). They'll be popping up from time to time as the main series progresses.

Now, my thank-yous...

Thank you so much to my Team Blackwood beta readers - Chandni, Ramona, Stanzin, Hence, Yusra, Jeff, Renata, Erazm, and Helen. You provided so much useful feedback on the first draft of this book, and I hope you can pick out the bits you mentioned in the final version.

Huge thanks to Abigail for making a beautiful cover

once again - I'm sure you must get sick of my "a bit darker, no, too dark, not dark enough" emails!

And to Amanda, my editor, for pointing out the plot gremlins and fixing my Britishisms, and Dominique and Emma, my proof readers.

And thanks to you for reading—I hope you stick around to meet the other characters fighting to get out of my head...

16731039R00141

Printed in Great Britain
by Amazon